The Hat Seller of Seville

Selected Short Stories and Poems

Phillip M Williams

This edition published in 2023
© 2023 Phillip M Williams

Published by Phillip M Williams
109 Mitchell Street
Merewether NSW 2291
Australia
swimwell.phil@gmail.com

National Library of Australia
Cataloguing-in-Publication entry

Williams, Phillip M.
The Hat Seller of Seville, Selected Short Stories and Poems

1st Ed.
ISBN 978-0-6456603-0-2

Acknowledgements

First and foremost, I thank Marie for her encouragement, feedback and editorial skills. She has been a loving and patient partner, humouring me when needed.

I've had great support and assistance from Garry Jennings, Bronwyn MacRitchie, Rebecca Trowbridge, Diana Pearce, Brian Noble, Penny Creighton, Ed Wright, Morgan Arnett.

Family and friends have been generous and genuine. I am grateful for their frank comments.

Scribes in my BoyzRite cadre, Hunter Writers Memoir Group and my colleagues in progressive writing have helped to shape my style.

Many people have urged me to publish this book. I thank them all, especially those who have read and responded to this collection of stories and poems.

Contents

The Hat Seller of Seville

Xavier Salazar's unique business plan paid dividends during the sweltering summer season in Seville. He purchased Bangladeshi-made hats from the wholesale market for E0.75 each and sold them for E5.00, cash only. His stock consisted of Panamas and Homburgs for men, and for ladies, Boaties and Trilbies.

Xavier was naturally handsome, slim with golden olive complexion. In summer the money he made by hawking sun hats to tourists meant he could take his Señora Attractivo to the Italian Alps in winter. Emilia's salary as a guard paid for the rent, food and mojitos. Eighty percent of Señor Salazar's sales came from tourists sitting on the open top deck of Seville's hop on/hop off City Sightseers Red Buses. Most passengers were Northern European, a sprinkling of Americans and a handful of Australians. Their peaches and cream complexions were easily burnt by the Andalucian sun.

On the day of the incident Xavier was wearing mustard slacks with tan belt, a pressed Iberian pink polo and brown leather loafers. His success as a salesman was partly due to his personal presentation, his wife Emilia ensuring that when 'her man' departed their small social housing unit, he was impeccably dressed. At the doorway on the third floor, she would always run her fingers through his voluminous black hair, combing it back before kissing him on the lips and wishing him 'buen dias mi hombre.'

There were no shade trees at Stop 14 on the Calle de Ancient Marinas. It was also the stop where drivers adjusted their time-table which often meant longer stays in scorching sun. This became the best place for Xavier to promote the benefits of his hats. The stop was half an hour from the city centre, time enough for visitors to begin feeling the heat and their faces to redden.

Xavier was not permitted onboard, instead he walked along the side of the bus holding the hats on one arm and showed five fingers with his other hand indicating the price. When a pas-senger nodded or said 'Si,' he would frisbee the hat upwards. If the hat was suitable, the purchaser would drop a five Euro note to finalise the transaction. Such was Xavier's skill that he never missed a sale, sometimes even running beside the bus after it had departed. The passing traffic never seemed to worry him when he worked the left hand side. But it wasn't always that simple. Fussy clients wished to change colour and some hats didn't fit, so a process of exchange was managed.

Often a five Euro note would flutter away from his out-stretched hand falling onto the road. Xavier, using the football skills he learnt in his youth, would effortlessly trap the note and then scoop it up without dropping any merchandise. Sometimes Xavier would need to provide change. This proved difficult for him because there was a gap of at least a metre between oppo-site outstretched hands. He mostly scrunched the note into a ball so that it would follow a straight trajectory for a simple catch. Sometimes he was able to dunk the note into an open lowered backpack. Infrequently the bus would depart without the change being successfully delivered. When this occurred he would enter the daily amount into his takings spreadsheet as 'miscellaneous', but also gave back the amount if the tourist returned later to ask for what was rightly theirs.

During tourist season buses stopped every twelve minutes, so from 10am to 3pm Xavier could provide his service to as many as 25 buses. If he sold 2 hats per bus, which was his average, then his profit for the day would be close to E250.00. It was good money for an unskilled worker in casual employment. Between buses, Xavier sat on a wooden stool under his sun umbrella amongst his boxed stock of hats and swigged his water canister. For sustenance he slurped three or four juicy Seville oranges a day.

One hot, humid afternoon in May the top deck was almost full and the usually sedate atmosphere was loud and raucous. Four overweight, sweaty young men, dressed in jeans and overly tight Union Jack T-shirts climbed the stairs and took the remaining four seats. In the manner of many arrogant young men on vacation, they began to talk loudly with liberal use of blasphemous language. Those sitting near to them turned away to avoid the noxious fumes of alcohol emanating from their breath and skin.

Upon seeing Xavier and his hats, they immediately wanted one each. Reaching well down the side of the bus exposing their rolled white flesh, they extended their hands to claim a white Panama each. But they did not pay, choosing instead to make a joke of it, claiming superiority of victory and joking about the gypsy hat seller. Xavier began to shout for his money, but the big red diesel bus chugged out into the traffic. The bovver boys laughed in self-congratulations.

But the incident had not gone unnoticed by others. A French Madame in the very back row was incensed by the young men's behaviour. She stood, remonstrated at them by pointing her parasol and scolded the rude boys, demanding they go back and honour the transaction. The piggiest of the poms turned around and raised his middle index finger in a demeaning gesture.

Silence followed.

At Stop 18, Xavier appeared at the top of the stairs. Behind him was a pretty, petite female Guardia Civil with full armoury – truncheon, handcuffs, pistol. Xavier pointed to the culprits. The officer walked to their seats. Motioning with her hands and addressing them in English.

'Stand up please.' The bovver boys did not move. She withdrew the truncheon from her belt and bought it down swiftly and sharply on the back of one the boy's hands which was gripping the seat in front.

'F**K!' he exclaimed, and immediately stood up. Another boy followed.

'Now you pay this man E20.00 each for your hats.'

Two boys looked at each other. Two sat and ignored her. The Guard spoke into her lapel microphone. Almost immediately she was joined to two burly male Guards who took positions behind her.

'You each pay E20.00 now, or we go to Prosecutor where you will stay overnight and pay much more.'

Two of the delinquents reached for their wallets and handed over the cash.

'Final time to ask,' she said authoritatively, as she pointed her cosh to the two recalcitrant miscreants.

One frisbeed his hat off the bus into the branches of a Plane Tree in an attempt to absolve himself from guilt. The Guardia Feminino stepped aside and nodded. Her burley male colleagues moved in, pulled the men up, handcuffed them and bundled them roughly down the steep stairs.

The other passengers saw the hooligans being kicked into the back of a Guardia Civil van below. There was applause all around, everybody happy that justice had been done and the 'nice hat seller' would get his money.

Xavier stood on the footpath with the female Guard. She passed the E40 already retrieved to the hat seller. They nodded to each other and went their own way, Xavier to climb the tree to retrieve the discarded Panama and thence to stop 14 to resume his work. The attractive Guardia Civil accompanied the drunk culprits to the prosecutor's office.

Back in their apartment that evening Xavier poured two mojitos as he lustily watched Emilia tease him as she took off her uniform. Firstly the thick black belt holding the truncheon, handcuffs and pistol was unbuckled and hung on the big hook behind the door. She undid her hair, throwing out the lustrous, jet black locks onto her shoulders and began to unbutton her serge navy shirt. Her long fingers probed into the top of her bra and she stealthily extracted two blue E20 notes, dangling them in front of him.

'Here is your money, Señor. A handsome profit for the handsome Hat Seller of Seville, si?'

Loving smiles came across both their faces. Xavier passed the mojito. 'Saludos' he greeted, as they clicked glasses.

Creative Writing

My grade five teacher, Mr Hatton simultaneously detected my dyslexia and destroyed any talent that I may have had for creative writing. Ralph Hatton was the crankiest teacher at the school with a fearsome reputation as an authoritarian. His voice boomed demanding attention like a sergeant major. Each day he wore a white shirt and black tie, often with a beige, home-knitted, over sized cardigan. He peered at us through his coke bottle glasses with thick black rims. These made his eyes appear enormous and monster-like. Hatton's homework task was to write a composition about a dIAry. Instead, I wrote about a dAIry.

I was pleased with my page and half description about milking cows, feeding poddy calves and separating cream. My writing was not copperplate, as he demanded, but the story line was strong and the dairy farmer and his wife were interesting characters. Or so I thought.

The composition books were handed back with corrections, comments and marks but mine was withheld. Mr Hatton asked me to come to the front of the class. For a fleeting second I thought that I was to be touted as the next Enid Blyton writing about The Secret Seven on a dairy farm. Instead I was introduced to my classmates as a dunce. He belittled me about my inability to discern diary from dairy.

'Williams can't even read properly, let alone write something as required.'

Hatton reached for the feather duster, his 'go-to' motivator for wayward students and told me to put my hand up. We'd all heard of his disciplinary methods from older boys like caning at will and chops with the edge of a ruler on the knuckles. This was to be my first experience of the cane and I was terrified. However much it hurt, I told myself not to cry, for that was a mark of weakness. I wanted to show Hatton that he needed more than two cuts to get the better of me because at the time I was secretly competing with Pinhead Simpson as the tough boy of the class. Pinhead was tall and lanky, the opposite of me, but his head was small compared to the rest of his body. It never crossed my mind that his nickname may have been demeaning.

'Get your hand up boy!'

I raised it to waist height. He urged it higher by pushing the back of my hand upwards with the cane. I turned my face away not wanting to see the horror. I noticed Pinhead sitting high at his desk observing every action. There was no sign of sympathy on his face.

'Swoosh' came the stick through the cool dusty classroom air. It was a sharp, wristy forehand flick and caught me unawares. I was expecting an axe swing. The sting hit me across the palm. I withdrew my hand to the safety of my pocket.

'Up again boy,' said the child abuser.

Swish, thwhack. It struck me across the end of my fingers. This time my eyes moistened, but I did not cry.

Pinhead was caned during his month as the ink monitor for inadvertently mixing the powdered ink in different shades of blue each week. This had the effect of making a composition book more like a Van Gogh masterpiece such were his hues of blue from navy to aquamarine. He sobbed for forty minutes and refused to look at me.

In term four Hatton became ill and 5A welcomed a replacement teacher. The classroom mood changed dramatically. Miss Phillips was warm, kind and encouraging. She placed a vase of fresh flowers on her desk, dressed in bright clothes and wore lipstick. She was the opposite of draconian Hatton. We all liked her soft voice and her humane approach to us as individuals.

Miss Phillips assigned us a composition task about 'The Storm.'

My opening line was 'Clouds rolled overhead.'

'What type of clouds were they Phillip?'

'Black clouds.'

'And how did the clouds look and feel to you? Were they threatening? About to explode with thunder and lightning?'

I nodded, delighted by my new teacher's suggestions and interest in me as a student.

'Were they ominous?' she said.

I did not know the word but nodded enthusiastically and began to write a new opening sentence. She helped me with spelling.

'Ominous black clouds thundered over head.'

'That's one of the best opening sentences I've ever seen for grade five.' Miss Phillips complimented me within earshot of Pinhead. I knew then that I could be a creative writer.

In the playground at recess we lined up for the one-third of a pint of free milk, courtesy of the Government. I made sure that I was in front of Pinhead in the line after the girls chose most of the strawberry or chocolate flavour leaving us with vomit-inducing banana milk.

Pinhead, his voice full of invective, called me a crawler.

I ignored him knowing that I was both tougher and brighter than he.

The Farmers' Wharf

My old man was a dock worker, after the war,
winching Bega Valley produce into holds of Illawarra Line
    Steamers at Tathra.
'The Pig and Whistle Line' coastal ships unloaded coal and cargo
    and
offered overnight passage to Sydney before tracks became roads.
The Captain waited for a pig, but not a minute after the whistle
    for a passenger.

In a howling black north-easterly with rising seas
the SS Kameruka steamed to a mooring buoy in the bay.
In the calm of next morning she made fast against huge spring-
    loaded buffers of the wharf.
I recall Dad in blue overalls striding into the cavernous warehouse.
I hear revving, smell the blue exhaust and watch the red Bedford
reverse to unload ironbark sleepers.

He winds the crane's jib, lowering boxed cheddar.
The freshening breeze tosses his blond curls.
Chop slaps the barnacled black hull of the ship.
Distracted by a sickening stink, I see dozens of pigs
squeal down the narrow gangway to their squalid sty on the stern
for their cruise to Darling Harbour abattoirs.

I clamber down slippery steep granite to the wet timber sub-deck
treading carefully to avoid painful piercings from
periwinkles, oysters and cart-rut shells.
Blue Pacific swell rolls beneath me before
crashing onto the boulders and squeezing into crevices and caves.

I lie prone on smooth weathered planks and
peer through the wide cracks as the sun singes my back.
Up-draughts of ocean breath freshen my face.
My fingers trace dark whorls in the wide grey planks.
I am mesmerised by the sway of kelp in the liquid sapphire way
    below.

Bass Strait Shenanigans

Dr Steven Kaminsky was ropable. His cherished silver bullet had been stolen, or so he claimed, and he wanted the Captain of the Coral Adventurer to find it. Kaminsky stormed onto the bridge and confronted the Captain who was taken aback by the rude intrusion during his afternoon watch. The theft, Kaminsky claimed, had occurred before lunch while the couple was hiking on Flinders Island and the ship was anchored off Trouser Point.

Kaminsky knew there was a 'no key' policy on this cruise meaning that cabins were not locked. But he had not deposited valuables with the Purser, as advised, because he liked to have the small missile with him for comfort. On this occasion he'd unintentionally left it on the bedside table. It was his security blanket, figuratively speaking. So much so that his wife Sandrine called the relationship between Kaminsky and his 'little toy' a classic case of psychological dependence.

Captain Smithers raised his eyebrows and his voice.

'Do you mean a *live* bullet, sir?'

'Well, uh, yes, in a fashion. It contains a propellant.'

The Captain stared at Kaminsky. 'Do you mean gun powder compressed in the cartridge?'

'More or less,' he replied.

'Do you realise that you've breached the Terms and Conditions of this cruise by bringing live ammunition aboard? Do you know that you've also committed an offence under Tasmanian Law?'

Kaminsky's head dropped at the severity of the Captain's allegations. Captain Smithers took up the phone and asked his Purser Mario to the Bridge. The smooth Italian from Sicily, experienced in dealing with difficult passengers would be much better placed to handle this situation.

'Mario, please accompany Dr Kaminsky to his cabin and begin a search of his room for a missing silver bullet. Let's start there.'

Captain Smithers swung his chair around to face the bow and took up binoculars as he navigated the ship towards Deal Island. He began to think about the situation. He somehow knew it would cause him and Kaminsky grief if the bullet were found, and maybe worse still if the bullet were not recovered.

The silver bullet had been presented for Kaminsky's 25 years of highly valuable work at the Australian Munitions Group (AMG) in Bendigo. He and his new, young and glamorous wife Sandrine were taking their first cruise since Kaminsky retired three months earlier. The unusual memento had been presented at his retirement dinner in recognition of his valuable contribution to the firm. Kaminsky had played a key part in the Strategic Development Team since he'd obtained his PhD in Chemistry from the University of Melbourne in 1991. He had a brilliant mind for molecules and atoms as they applied to gunpowder and propulsive mixtures. He was a key member of a small team of scientists spearheading the testing of ammunition prototypes such as tank disabling armaments, bombs and missiles.

Mario followed the troubled passenger into cabin 517 on the starboard side, when Kaminsky demanded:

'It is not one of the passengers that has taken my jewel, but one of your crew! I want you to start with the ones who clean my room, then systematically search all others.'

Mario asked Kaminsky to retrace his activities from the time he dressed to when he realised the bullet was missing. Kaminsky admitted that he'd forgotten to put it in his pocket before disembarking for the day's hike. He always slept with the bullet next to him on the bedside table.

After a thorough search of the cabin for no result, Mario returned to his office and pulled up the intranet to view the morning's cleaning roster for the level 5 cabins.

❖

There was no history of kleptomania in her family, although a first fleet ancestor had been found guilty of stealing a sheep and was sent to Van Diemen's land in 1824. It was hardly a genetic trait, but Shannon's tendency to take small items of jewellery worried her mother Gwendolyn. Since primary school her daughter had often been caught with other people's baubles.

It was Shannon's grandmother who alerted Gwendolyn after Nanna's jewellery box was pilfered. Gwendolyn found the ring in four-year old Shannon's pocket the next day. The child had refused to admit she had taken it. Despite admonishment, there was no repentance from Shannon. Over time, other items disappeared from Nanna's small but valuable box when the granddaughter visited her Nanna.

A pattern of thieving developed. Small expensive adornments were taken from friends and neighbours houses. Shannon was asked to leave secondary school in Year 10 after the parents of one child called the police. Their daughter accused Shannon of not returning a precious pendant that was 'borrowed' for a weekend's outing. The accusers did not press charges but it was serious enough for Shannon's parents to seek psychological intervention.

During the course of counselling Shannon admitted she did not take things out of malice or jealousy, but simply because she found it comforting to have something in her pocket with which to fondle. She found the shapes intriguing and the smooth texture of metal relieved her anxiety. Best of all were small, heavy items. Knowing that she had stolen them added intrigue and excitement.

Gwendolyn took her teenage daughter on a cruise thinking that time away from her environment might cure this 'childish fetish.' On board Shannon met some other young people who worked on the ship. They encouraged her to 'join up' because life on a cruise liner was exciting, her accommodation and food was provided and she could save most of her pay.

She began as a cabin attendant aboard the Coral Adventurer, one of the ships in the Coral Expeditions fleet. In the first year, she cruised the Barrier Reef, Kimberley Coast and Sulawesi archipelago. She met many engaging people, made good friends and loved the job. But her suppressed urge to steal was challenged each time she entered cabins to clean while guests were on shore.

Despite the earlier course of behavioural therapy, she couldn't help but take a heavy solid-silver sea-dragon brooch from the cabin on the Bridge Deck, level 6, the most expensive cabins of all. She knew the owner, an attractive middle-aged lady travelling with a 'sugar-daddy,' as her friends called him. It was Shannon's boldest theft and she knew that her job would be on the line if anyone found out.

But there was no report filed by the rich couple and Shannon moved on to her next cruise. By this time she was 22 years old and having a great time socially, both on board and on-shore with workmates. Shannon was amazed at the volume of expensive jewellery left in the cabins as she vacuumed and tidied around the treasures. She resisted taking all but one thing on each cruise. In that way, it was more likely her illicit behaviour would go undetected.

She was intrigued with a silver bullet left on the bedside table in cabin 517. When she picked it up she swooned at its weighty density, the perfectly smooth cylindrical shape of the cartridge and the pointy tip of the bullet. It was the best feeling she'd experienced from a 'found object' as Shannon now called her 'objects de larceny.' She rolled it in her fingers amazed by its tactility, but slightly confused by a series of indentations around the cartridge case.

When she returned to her cabin Shannon examined the trophy. The indentations were letters, and as she rolled the bullet in her fingers she read,

To Dr Kaminsky
with gratitude & respect
AMG

❖

Mario interviewed three staff members, one of whom was Shannon who admitted that she had cleaned cabin 517 that morning. Yes, she had seen the bullet because it was such an unusual item. Yes, she had lifted it in order to wipe the table free of dust but returned it as she'd found it. No, she hadn't taken it.

But Mario noticed that her eyes looked away when she spoke the final sentence. Mario suspected that she was guilty, but he liked Shannon, not just because she was a good employee, but because of her engaging personality. Even if she did happen to take the small object, it was not a sacking offence, in his view.

The Head Purser knocked on the door of Cabin 517 just

before drinks at 6pm. He reported to Kaminsky that his enquiries had come to an end and suggested that Kaminsky himself had lost the bullet. After all, Kaminsky and his glamorous wife had been hiking each day across beaches and up steep inclines. Maybe he'd forgotten to zip the pocket in which the bullet lay.

'By the way,' Mario asked, 'if you carry the bullet with you and you accidentally fall on the granite slope, would the impact detonate the missile?'

There was a silence between the two men. Mario's uncle was a member of the Mafia and had taught a young Mario about holding steely facial expressions to intimidate opponents. Mario's eyes did not move from Kaminsky's face until Mrs Kaminsky appeared beside her husband, dressed extravagantly for dinner.

'Hello Mario, I met you briefly when we boarded. I'm Sandrine, Kaminsky's wife. I understand that you're helping Kaminsky locate his little bullet? You know he loses it often at home and it always shows up in one of his pockets.'

Mario returned his glare to Kaminsky, raising his eyebrows, expecting an answer.

'There is a slight possibility that it may go off, yes, but the chances are very slim. I know about bullets and I can take care in managing them. Someone has stolen it. It is quite valuable to me. If you cannot find it then I will be taking legal action against the company.'

Kaminsky's attitude and arrogance annoyed Mario. Dr Kaminsky was a small man with thick glasses and thin lips; not that Mario would judge someone's character by their appearance. Mario did wonder about the attraction he offered to the voluptuous Sandrine?

❖

Late that evening Mario went to the bridge and reported his findings to the Captain as the Coral Adventurer plied northward in heavy seas.

'This is a difficult situation Mario, because we have potentially lethal ammunition on board, its location unknown, and we have a passenger who has broken the law to bring it aboard. We need to locate it very quickly and bring the matter to a satisfactory conclusion. I want you to speak privately to Kaminsky's wife and ask her to search the cabin and his clothes. Then I want you to speak with Shannon and go with her to her bunkhouse and search her things.'

Mario located Shannon who was clearing up in the dining room. He took her to the outside deck where they both stood next to the railing. Shannon knew that she had been busted. He began by telling her a story.

'When I was a boy in Sicily I had to make a decision between joining my uncles who were members of a Mafia gang, or leaving the Island and living an honest life. I knew that if I joined my uncle and his murderous friends then I would not be able to live with myself. I did not want to ruin other people's lives, I wanted to enhance them. I adopted honesty, integrity and respect as my core values.'

He looked at Shannon and paused, waiting for his words to sink in. She was looking across the blue swell and white-capped waves to the horizon.

'Now we will go to your room and you will allow me to search your things for a missing sliver bullet. If there is nothing, it will be fine and we get along as before. If we find something that you shouldn't have, then we talk again.'

They entered the tiny room that Shannon occupied on level

3, below the water line. She went directly to her cupboard, rummaged around in a duffle bag and withdrew a red velvet purse-string bag. Mario followed her movement to the bed where Shannon opened the bag, turned it upside down and revealed the contents as silver trinkets clinked and clunked onto the coverlet. There was the sea-dragon brooch, a Mercedes Benz logo, a delicate necklace, three rings with various stones, a bracelet, a designer watch and in the middle of the pile, the silver bullet. All of Shannon's pirated booty from the high seas of Bass Strait aboard the cruise ship Coral Adventurer.

Not a word was said between Head Purser Mario and Cabin Attendant Shannon as they looked at each other in the small cramped crew quarters. Mario reached down and plucked the silver bullet from the bed. Shannon began to sob.

Mrs Kaminsky was ushered to the Purser's office at breakfast. Mario greeted her with a stunning smile and asked her to sit opposite him as the door closed. He had Italian charisma in spades when he wanted and Sandrine was pleasantly disarmed by his manner, not to mention his pressed white shirt with gold-braided, navy epaulettes. She left his office with a plan to assist the investigation and with Mario's private phone number, promising him that she would call when his roster finished in May. Maybe they could catch up? Mario had suggested.

Sandrine hurried to the cabin and before her husband returned from breakfast, slipped the bullet into the pocket of Kaminsky's Kathmandu jacket zipping it tightly. She ensured that her husband wore the jacket that day for their hike to Castle Rock. En route from ship to shore on the landing craft, Dr Kaminsky unzipped his pockets to keep his hands warm. He then produced the bullet and held it up for his wife to see with a look of surprise and happiness. She nodded and smiled, as if to say, 'I told you so, you silly man.'

Late that evening, Mario asked Shannon to bring her purse of stolen items to his cabin. From there, they went to the side deck.

'You can seek redemption now Shannon, by casting this bag into the sea. When you discard these things, you will be free of your impulse to steal and you will be free of guilt. You will not be penalised by this company. It is just between you and me. You will keep your job. Be true to yourself Shannon, that is the most important thing in life.'

Mario's Catholic upbringing shone through, despite the family's Mafia connection. He was far from the priestly type, but he was the shining beacon for pastoral care for the young employees of Coral Expeditions. With the throw of a test cricketer from the boundary, Shannon discarded the draw string purse and its contents into the waters of Bass Strait.

Mario reported to the Captain that the matter was resolved. The bullet had been located and was now in a safe custody box to be returned to Dr Kaminsky on disembarkation. Shannon had been disciplined and counselled. The Captain was satisfied that Mario had taken it upon himself to act as her mentor during her development with the company.

◆

Mario, home in Cairns on a four-week holiday, allowed the phone to ring out because he didn't recognise the caller. It was 5pm and the voice message was from Sandrine. Her sweet, playful voice implored a meeting. 'Hello Mario, it's Sandrine here. Remember the silver bullet shenanigans? I'm in Cairns to see the Barrier Reef. I'd love to catch up with you. I'm staying at the Shangri-La. I'm with a girl friend beside the pool. I'd love to buy you a cocktail. Please ring me on this number. Bye.'

Constitution Dock

Tourists returning to Salamanca and the Waterfront
seek colonial pubs for pints, fish and fries
markets purvey seafood, bread and wine.
Trawlers, lobster boats and long-liners prepare for
Storm Bay's scallops, squid and salmon despite
perfidious squalls and seas.

Yachts slumber in floating trances while
tars untangle rigging on tall ships.
Barques and brigs hold tight
to timber finger wharves, their
peace penetrated by gulls demanding hot chips.

Imposing sandstone edifices rim the dock perimeter
customs, courts, churches and clocks
dictated citizenry life in colonial times and exerted
British power in wild Van Dieman's Land.

Puffed and pimped statues of invader males
posture on elevated plinths.
Governors, admirals, reverends and explorers with
chests out, chins high, in
deceptive edification.

No public recognition for Truganini nor
apology for the massacres
no acknowledgement of the tribes no longer with us
nothing about the Black Line policy of systemic murder
except for museum exhibits displayed as prizes of the invasion.

Gypsy Woman

It was Sunday morning at the Ocean Baths when I first saw her. She was impossible to ignore because she stood out in a tableau so strikingly different from the usually mundane weekend scene. I positioned myself on the concrete walkway between the beach and the children's pool to observe her antics. Flouncing furtively in a tight swimsuit and seemingly unaware of people gawking at her, she twirled a white hoop around her waist and another around her left wrist, swaying to lively gypsy tunes emanating from her ancient tape deck.

Her hula-hooping was as polished as any gymnast. For someone like me, with time on his hands, it was entertaining to wile away an hour or two in the warm sunshine. Toddlers abruptly stopped and stared, forcing their parents to pause for another gander. Some of the little ones began to dance to the tuneful violin music. A crowd of 20 or 30 onlookers encircled her, smiling at each other and commenting on the seemingly effortless skill of her hoop work. Sun-worshipping, tattooed teenagers, sprawled on towels sat cross-legged along the concourse videoing her for an Insta post.

'She's so, like, cool and retro,' announced one, while taking a selfie. 'But she has too much silver jewellery, it's just way over-the-top,' referring to the Gypsy Woman's large earrings and bangles.

'Oooh I loooove the leopard skin one-piece,' the other giggled, as she palmed sunscreen over her buttocks and thighs while avoiding the straps of her white G-string.

Shuffling along in their thongs and speedos towards the big lap pool, regulars peered at her. Some frowned, frustrated by the crowded walkway. Others smiled, refreshed by such a dazzling newcomer. Crusty old-timers in faded budgie smugglers sitting on the steps near the change rooms scrutinised her, shaking their heads and tut-tutting.

Next to the tape deck lay a faded beach towel, over-stuffed straw bag and a plastic water bottle guarded by an alert, collarless Jack Russell who was squat on his haunches assessing everybody who came near. A disarray of hoops lay nearby with a hand written sign on cardboard: 'Hoops $5.00'

Five foot two in the old system with thick, shoulder length auburn hair and liquid black eyes sparkling like the water in the rock pools, she was beguiling and striking. Her stout legs and thick body were taut, fit and strong and in her unique Romani way, she was, to me, sexy and mysterious.

It was now after 10.00am and the sun was warming. After taking a swig of water she stepped out of her hoops and non-chalantly swaggered to the pool edge and dived in, swimming underwater halfway across the pool. Upon return, she scooped up her towel, wiped the water from her pretty face and smiled at me.

'I'm really enjoying your hula-hooping. You're very good at it.'

'Thank you Sir. I've been doing it a long time and I use it for fitness and meditation. Being near the water like this makes it really special.'

'Where did you learn? Are you self-taught,' I asked.

'Circus performing is part of my family so I learnt a lot from cousins and aunties. My parents also sent me to Circus Avalon for a year and that helped me polish up some routines. My name's Lulu by-the-way,' and she offered me her firm hand.

'I'm Phil, Lulu. Pleased to meet you.'

Lulu smiled and turned on the tape deck to begin another performance. With her hair drenched and water dripping from her costume she took up a handful of hoops and began a more exotic routine. The colourful hoops spun unerringly around and around, side to side, up and down, her body moved effortlessly and rhythmically.

I never considered her to be busking even though her wide brimmed beach hat lay upside down on the perimeter of her unmarked space. Perhaps she was inviting donations of coins in appreciation of her act. Whether the hat was placed or fell to this position is a moot point. To me, she was showcasing an exercise routine in the same way the morning lap swimmers, the boot camp captives or the stair-running obsessives do along the beach strip.

Two small children, holding hands, ran up to the hat and threw in some gold coins. Lulu smiled at them and looked for the parents to nod her appreciation. More coins were tossed, more people smiled and many more were compelled to move when the tape played La Bomba as Lulu expertly played the crowd through her guile, music and movement.

Suddenly, the spell of the dance was broken by an intrusion on the periphery of my vision. A Council Compliance Officer strode purposefully toward Lulu. He wore a yellow vest, wide brimmed brown hat, long pants and from his belt dangled several electronic devices. The contrast between the Officer and Lulu could not have been more stark. He took a camera from his pocket and photographed the dance, her possessions and the crowd. The Jack Russell's hackles were raised and he growled threateningly. Stepping forward, arms folded, he said to her:

'Can I see your busking permit please?'

Lulu opened her arms, turned towards the crowd, smiled and in a loud theatrical voice:

'Permit? Really?'

It was a perfect way for her to garner support. People murmured, shuffled their feet and awaited the Inspector's response. Lulu swaggered across the unmarked space to distance herself from the Council regulator. The Officer was stranded, unused to challenge and chagrin. I asked, from my position on the railing, if there was a problem.

'We've had a complaint about this woman blocking access to the pool with her busking. She needs a permit if she's conducting business here. She can apply to Council with her ABN and a copy of her Public Liability Insurance, and we'll assess its merits.'

'And this dog needs to be restrained and removed from this dog-free area, otherwise I'll impound it,' he continued, trying to gain control of the situation by threat and intimidation.

'It sounds like a lot of bureaucratic nonsense to me,' I said. 'Here's a woman doing her morning exercise regime, the people are enjoying watching her and no-one is being harmed. In fact, it's the opposite. Everyone is loving it. We're all happy.'

'Rules are rules mate. There are Local Government Regulations that have to be complied with. I'm just doing my job.'

'Why don't you go up onto the footpath and give out a few tickets to people who let their dogs poo on the walkway and don't pick it up? And what about the people who park in the disabled parking zones when they clearly aren't disabled or don't have a sticker?'

Lulu, unperturbed, hooped effervescently around the walkway keeping her distance, happy to be playing second fiddle. A young mother, a babe on her hip and a toddler holding her hand, came forward.

'We love her. She is so good and my kids are engrossed. Please don't spoil it.'

Two broad-chested, bearded men in board shorts sidled up, arms folded as in defiance of the regulator. We stood as a protest group while the gathering throng clapped Lulu and swayed along with her to the strings of a gypsy fiddler and a swooning male vocalist. Then a very brown, wrinkled, tattooed older man in rugby shorts stepped forward to address the officer.

'Don't you think the Council's done enough to piss people off? You work for us you know, and none of us here want to see anything happen to that young lady.'

He pointed to Lulu who by this time was returning from her sashaying. The Council officer turned and strode away, his enforcement devices bouncing from his belt. He had driven his HiLux with flashing orange lights down onto the concourse as if it were an emergency.

'Thank you sooo much for your support,' said Lulu as she gathered up her hat and coins.

'Can I help you with your stuff?' I asked, while scooping up the hoops. We chatted as we headed for the car park until we came to her Old Suzuki Jimny.

Lulu and I became friends after that morning at the pool. I visited her at her little caravan on a private block up near the airport. A sign on the main road indicated her hideaway: 'JEWELLERY FOR SALE'. The mail box was stacked with egg cartons and scrawled on Styrofoam in black Texta: 'Free range organic eggs $6.00'. A weather-beaten Arnott's biscuit tin served as the honesty box.

A sympathetic farmer, Stan, provided the site for free. An electrical lead ran through the kikuyu to her tiny wooden van. Black and brown hens fussed and scratched through the long grass in free-range bliss. A Persian rug lying on the ground under a canvas awning created a comfortable patio. The distinctive aroma of a mosquito coil lazily swirled from under the weather beaten camp table.

The arrangement with Stan suited Lulu because she had no income apart from a Centrelink benefit and cash that she might earn from her hooping. During summer she worked her way from the North, down the coast to Newcastle and then back up to Urunga as autumn approached. From experience, she'd found hooping locations in seaside holiday towns a good cash cow.

Lulu always insisted on me having a cup of tea from her small samovar and a golden-topped, flat scone with butter and home made blackberry jam. I always looked forward to the mouth watering afternoon tea and I found it hard to limit myself to one scone.

'My Nonna taught me to make scones,' she said. 'I've been baking them twice a week. The proper recipe from Albania used sheep milk, but that is hard to get here, so I use milk from Stan's beautiful Jersey. Stan always gets his share – I call them rent cakes,' she giggled.

Lulu was always up for a chat, each of us slumped in her camp chairs sipping from chipped enamel mugs. Alvin, the Jack Russell guard, dutifully perched beside her until she tapped her thigh and he would jump effortlessly to settle across her lap to be stroked. His eyes never left me and I knew from his look not to mess with him or Lulu.

I learnt much about her interesting life. Her name was Luludja Argentari (which means Silversmith in Romani). Her Grandparents migrated to Australia in 1952 and became roaming hawkers across the countryside, just as they'd done in Albania. As a girl, she spent school holidays with them while learning to sing, dance and cook from her Nonna and how to work silver from her Papa.

One late summer afternoon I drove down the dirt track, but

her camp was gone. There was no sign of the caravan, Jimny, Alvin, chickens or jewellery. I was disappointed but I knew it was inevitable. Stan shouted and waved from his house across the paddock and began to walk across.

'She's gone, on her way home, next stop up at Nelson Bay. Asked me to give you these.' He held out a brown paper bag.

'The Council kept hassling her about the busking so she knew it was time to go. It happens everywhere. Why can't they just leave us alone and let us get on with our lives?'

I peeped inside the bag to find two Albanian scones, two brown eggs and a handmade card written in a flourishing green ink.

> *Goodbye my friend & always remember*
> *Not all those who wander are lost.*
> *Lulu xxx*

Manta Ray

```
             fin          tips
                cut       the
             aqua            marine
        silky surface as she cruises carefree and
      curious  s c a n n i n g  my alien body propelled
     by one silent  powerful  swoop  of  triangular  wings
     horn - shaped   lobes   f u n n e l   water  into   a
       g a p i n g   m o u t h  as she glides by casting a
         diamond-shaped  shadow  on  the  palette of
            coral below I am m e s m e r i s e d
               her   stunning   sleek   skin
               glistens e x q u i s i t e l y
                    in  the  pristine
                    P a c i f i c
                          ~
                          ~
                          b
                          l
                          u
                          e
```

Facebook Prototype 1960

My father's face is lit by a yellow glow from gauges and instrument panels. A large microphone sits on the middle of his bench in the 'radio hut' underneath the house. One wall is covered in 'postcards' sent from exotic locations from his 'Facebook' friends. On another wall is a map of the world. Above his operating bench are photos of warships.

This was a place for my brother and I. We'd run down the back wooden steps and swing under the patio into a cabin filled with electronics and intrigue. There was muted light in his shack and the smoke from his Ardath cork-tipped cigarettes stung our eyes. It was as if we'd been transported into a ship's radio room.

He'd switched on the valves of his Ham Radio fifteen minutes earlier to warm up 'the set' which was a series of home made boxes, stacked one on top of the other, housing valves, condensers and coloured wires. Switches, dials and gauges were all within his reach. Covering nearly each side of his head were imposing HMV ear phones. Then he'd broadcast to the world.

CQ CQ CQ

This is VK 2AYW, testing, testing, testing.

Victor King Two Alpha Yankee Whiskey testing.

VK2 AYW, is anybody there? Over.

The CQ call was an invitation to others who were listening in that frequency to respond.

My Dad explained that his voice would be transmitted up the wire above the house and out into the atmosphere through the aerial. Weeks before he had mates from the RSL help him erect a tall, straight sapling to anchor the wire from the chimney of the house. It traversed across our backyard and was visible from the main street.

His mates from the club knew him as Jack, the ex Chief Petty Officer from fourteen years in the Royal Australian Navy. He knew about call signs, frequencies and band widths from his days on the His Majesty's Australian Ships the Bungaree, Sydney and Quickmatch. We read the faded carbon copied messages he'd deciphered from morse code. On board the HMAS Perth in September 1939 when the ship was in port at Kingston Jamaica he ran from the radio room to the bridge and handed the Captain the grave message.

Commence hostilities at once with Germany. Neville Chamberlain, PM, British High Command

In 1960 he'd begun a hobby with amateur or Ham radio, operating in short wave frequency bands. With the call sign VK 2AYW his goal was to have a yarn with other radio amateurs around the world, to relive his naval days and build up some friends around the globe. Just like Facebook, except the communication was aural, not written, and there were no photos.

We'd crowd around his desk, careful not to bump apparatus or trip on live electrical leads. My big brother Terry and I peeled our eyes on the yellow frequency dial and our ears were eager for a 'pickup' response. As Dad delicately tuned the dial we followed the needle on the round screen until we heard a crackling voice from the stratosphere.

As the American accent spoke slowly, my Dad would fine tune the dial to gain clarity of voice and write the call sign on his scribble pad. Depressing the button on the microphone, he'd reply.

'Hello K4 APT. This is VK 2AYW calling from Bega, Australia.

Jack Williams operating. Thanks for the pick up K4 APT. Do you read me K4 APT? Over.'

Terry and I watched and listened intently, eagerly awaiting a good hook up.

'VK 2AYW. Hello Jack, this is Vince Zettervall, in Duluth, Minnesota. Pleased to have the hook-up with you Buddy. You're loud and clear Jack. I don't get a lot of hook ups from Down Under with our different time zones and weather. But we've got a beautiful winter night here, minus 20 degrees and clear skies. I'm operating from my shack on the edge of the woods next to Lake Superior with five feet of snow outside. Over.'

We looked at each other with wide eyes. It was hard to imagine a little log cabin amongst a pine forest half buried in snow and a man speaking to us from America. We were in shorts, singlets and thongs.

'K4 APT. This is VK 2AYW. Nice to hear your voice Vince. Your signal is loud and clear. I've got two young boys listening. Sunday morning here is warm and sunny. We'll be going to the beach after breakfast. What sort of gear are you operating? Over.'

The conversation continued between Dad and Vince as Terry and I tried to find Duluth on the coloured map of the world nailed with clouts to the thin masonite wall. For every 'hookup,' Dad would place a coloured pin in the towns of countries across the globe. We had no idea where Minnesota was until Dad alerted us to North America.

It was my first lesson in geography and over time I leant about the continents and islands as well as capital cities, rivers and mountain ranges. Along with Dad's photo albums of his naval days we saw the world through Dad's 'Facebook' friends. It ignited my passion for travel.

The two men from the opposite ends of the earth continued to chat about radio gear and their history as Ham operators.

They compared notes about their lives, families and war service. Names and addresses were swapped and invitations to come and visit 'at any time' were extended. Promises were made to 'hook up' again next month. But that didn't seem to happen. My Dad was keener to find another amateur radio enthusiast in Scandinavia, Africa, or even a remote part of Australia. He wanted to show us how many pins he could display on his map.

He wanted to have as many 'Likes' on his 'Facebook' page as he could manage.

The Roger Milsom Chronicles

Do you have a passion?

The looming job interview during lockdown did not really suit Roger. His previous successful interviews were person-to-person, where he could present his whole self, not just his visage on a screen. Zoom, Roger thought, would not allow him to display his full 'magnetismo.'

Roger Milsom was old-school. Despite trepidation with the new technology, he presented himself dressed as he would for a 'proper' interview, in front of a panel – crisp white shirt, striped blue tie, smart jacket, creased slacks and polished black shoes.

Since his face would be the only feature showing, he took considerable care to shave cleanly and closely, clip errant nostril hairs and not over-use the pomade. He cleaned his glasses so that the tortoise-shell rims gleamed and there were no smudge marks or finger imprints on the lenses.

Throughout life, Roger had wholeheartedly adopted one of his mother's adages: 'Honesty is the best policy.' He could not abide people being 'flexible with the truth.' If he suspected anyone being dishonest he would challenge them. Consequently, he had few friends, often offending people with his assertive manner. He was far from aggressive but sometimes lacked diplomacy.

Roger kept himself occupied outside of work hours with his passion – toy trains. In his parents' double garage he'd established an impressive track network. One passenger and two freight train sets set ran simultaneously along 150 metres of interlocking track. He'd spend weekends there manoeuvring the trains and adjusting stations, signals and overpasses.

After logging in to the Zoom link, Roger could see the three interviewers' faces and the shock of his own. He quickly moved back from the screen and adjusted his glasses. Predictable questions came forward. 'Where do you see yourself in five years' time? Why do you think you're the right person for this job?'

Roger felt that he'd answered all the questions competently, as he'd prepared diligently for different scenarios. The interview panel members nodded and smiled at him, as if he was doing well. But he was not prepared for the final question, asked by the Head of HR.

'Do you have a passion Roger?' It was so unexpected that it threw him momentarily, he lost concentration and began to mumble.

Roger was embarrassed. By admitting a passion for toy trains, he may be perceived as a fuddy-duddy and not suitable for this role. On the other hand, he was proud of his hobby and did not want to disavow an important pillar of his life. He wanted to be honest. Leaning toward the screen he pulled the lapel of his jacket toward the camera. The interviewers saw the badge – a British Green Steam Loco.

'I'm a toy train nerd,' Roger uttered. His cheeky grin revealed his boyish enthusiasm.

Roger Milsom was offered the job.

Warm regards

In her fifteen years of work as a legal secretary, Susan Beveridge had never seen a work-related email signed off as 'Warm regards.' Usually it was 'Yours sincerely,' followed by the full name of the correspondent and their position in the organisation. In some cases, the letter writer would include their qualifications and memberships.

Susan had never changed her 'sign-off.' In fact her email signature was, more or less, pre-determined and provided by the Legal Department as:

Yours sincerely
Susan Beveridge
S.R. Beveridge
Legal Secretary
EASTCAP

Susan had successfully negotiated with Mr Price (now deceased), one of the firm's partners responsible for 'Protocol' at the time, to have her first name used in the signature, not just a gender-free, sterile 'S.' Mr Price had also agreed for her to use a Brush Script font, in bold. Susan wanted her correspondents to know that they were dealing with a woman.

In the matter at hand, Susan was liaising with the HR Department about the adoption of new policies and procedures. How unusual that the 'liaison' was conducted electronically and not face-to-face, especially from HR since they were just four floors below, thought Susan.

Susan was shaken by the sign off email signature:

Warm regards
Roger M
Roger Milsom
Employee Relationship Liaison Officer
EASTCAP

B.Ec (Syd) Dip. Eng. Member T.T.A. NSW

As she was sipping her first glass of refreshing Sauvignon-Blanc while preparing a Greek Salad to accompany the salmon for a summer night's meal, Susan pondered Roger Milsom's email signature She began to note the issues that were well outside EASTCAP's 'Protocol Guidelines.'

In addition to 'Warm regards,' the sign-off was situated on the right hand margin. Secondly, the stylised signature was first name and a capital only for the surname. She wondered too, why a man with an economics degree and an engineering diploma would be working in HR? And 'TTA?'What on earth was the script? Was Roger a calligrapher?

After topping up her Sauv Blanc, Susan opened her computer and logged into EASTCAP's Home Page. Scrolling through the staff profiles and photographs of all those who worked in 'Head Office' at Darling Harbour she discovered that Roger Milsom was not listed! Disappointed and distracted as she was by 'Roger M,' she tried to take in the ABC News and 7.30 Report. She never missed Leigh Sales or Laura Tingle, considering their acerbic interrogations of politicians 'must watch' TV.

At her desk at 9.30am the next morning an email appeared from Roger Milsom, wanting to know if she had received the document and to let him know if there were questions or issues. He'd signed off again with 'Warm regards,' as if he knew her and liked her. It was unconventional, to say the least.

'How interesting,' thought Susan. 'The document arrived at 4.00pm yesterday and he was chasing up a response early the next morning. How little he knew about how the Legal Section worked!'

She waited until 4.30pm that afternoon to reply.

Dear Mr Milsom,
It is unlikely you'll have a response from the Legal Department
on an HR issue for some time due to an unprecedented heavy
workload on mergers and acquisitions. I will notify you of our
advice at the appropriate time.
Warm regards
Susan Beveridge
PS Roger, I can't find your details on the HR Staff Profile?

Susan justified her 'sign-off' because the response was internal, Roger was not a 'real' client, just a colleague, and she wanted to play with him. Almost immediately Roger's reply pinged on her screen.

Lo Susan
Thanks for alerting me to my missing staff profile. I'll attend to it.
                                        Very warm regards
                                                    Roger

There's something about Roger

On Monday in her office on the 12th floor, Susan Beveridge was preparing agenda papers for the Mergers and Acquisitions Committee when she noticed the arrival of an email. Normally, in the course of best office practice, she would not interrupt her work to open an email. 'Always complete the task you're working on before beginning a new one.' It was a mantra that had stayed with her since her school days at St Scholastica.

But Susan had glanced at the screen, noticing the sender was Roger Milson. In her hands were nine copies of a proposal recommending the takeover of a small mutual building society. Her task at hand was to insert the proposal into each of 9 bundles so that the papers could be distributed by the close of business that day. It was now 4.45pm.

She knew the St Scholastica Nuns would be furious at her for choosing to open the message and neglecting a more important task. Placing the pile of papers at the end of her desk, Susan sat in front of her computer. *Bugger the Nuns and bugger Catholic guilt.*

Lo Susan
Very pleased to advise you that I've managed to upload my profile on the staff intranet.
Now you'll know who you're dealing with!
Have you made any progress on HR's request to M &A?

Highest regards
Roger M

For some reason, she'd become intrigued by this new member of staff and his unusual fonts, right alignment sign-off and unorthodox email signature. Who was Roger Milsom and why wasn't he following the company's Style Guide?

Susan clicked on Roger's profile at 4.50pm. She was immediately struck by the headshot. Was it his confident pose, natural smile or thick black tresses? He had a certain presence, confidence and attraction.

'Who's that handsome man Susan? I do like his butt chin, do you? He looks so much like John Travolta, don't you think?'

'Oh you scared me Imogen, sorry. This is the new guy in HR. Have you met him yet?'

Susan leant toward the screen to explore Roger's cleft. Not so much a cleft, she thought, more a dimple.

'You know what they say about men with a cleft chin don't you?' asked Imogen. And without waiting for a response said, 'it means they want a personal connection with you. Now, where are the agenda papers?'

'Oh, don't be so silly Imogen!' Susan was annoyed with herself that she'd allowed her emotional interest in Roger to overtake her usually reliable and efficient work. Perhaps the Nuns were right?

Susan quickly attended to the agendas then handed them to Imogen. It was 5.05pm before Susan began to read Roger's brief biography. He was on her mind on the 324 Bus to Rose Bay and again as she sipped her wine in her apartment wondering whether to cook or order Uber Eats.

At the same time across the city Roger walked his two rescue greyhounds, Betsy and Bob. He'd adopted the pair two years ago and they were now an integral part of his life. In his semi-detached brick home beside the railway line in Summer Hill, they slept in their own orthopaedic dog beds in his bedroom and spent the daytime in the small backyard while he was at work.

Most evenings after dinner, they accompanied Roger to the train garage to watch their revered owner manoeuvre his toys. He'd constructed a well cushioned settee using milk crates to position the bench high enough for the dogs to enjoy the rhythm and transit of the railway cars. Betsy quickly became bored, preferring to doze. Bob, on the other hand watched intently as the locos roared past, following each set with his stereoscopic ears.

Susan was trying to concentrate on the detail of the 7.30 Report that evening because one of the segments was about Barnaby Joyce. He was of interest to her, not so much because of his politics, but because of his philandering. But even Barnaby could not keep Susan's mind away from Roger.

There was something about Roger.

Roger's Raffle

To: Susan Beveridge
Subject: Roger Milsom
From: HR Sweetenham

Hello Susan
We've had to let Roger go, he's no longer with us. Please direct
your communications regarding HR matters to me until we find
a suitable replacement going forward.
Regards
Hal Sweetenham
Director, Human Relations
EASTCAP

How Susan hated 'corporate speak' and euphemisms like 'let go' instead of sacked or fired! And, OMG, as for 'Going Forward.' But at least Hal Sweetenham was aligned left and had used the proper font.

Susan was peeved because she'd not had the opportunity to meet Roger. Naturally inquisitive and determined, she wanted to know more, especially if he was married. Susan admitted to herself that she found him alluring in a wholesome way. There weren't many men like him anymore and at 28 years of age Susan was feeling the need to find a male partner.

'Hello Hal, nice to see you. We don't see you enough on level 12.'

Susan took a sip of her champagne. She knew that Hal Sweetenham always liked after-work drinks on Friday night at the Pumphouse Bar in the Novotel.

'Can I ask you about Roger Milsom? He wasn't with us for long. What happened?'

'I can't tell you a thing Susan, you know about confidentiality. All I can say is that Roger spent too much time on non-work related activities during work hours. We had to let him go even though he'd been warned.'

Susan knew that Hal could be provoked, especially when he'd a drink or two. And Hal was a sucker for charming, attractive women.

'Come on Hal. It's a bit unusual isn't it for someone to be sacked so soon after appointment. Did you make a mistake in the recruitment process?'

'Well, Roger spent a lot of time administering his hobby during work hours. He's a toy train enthusiast and it was obvious that was more important to him than his job with us. A bit obsessive, if you ask me. Lovely man but ... '

With her glass of wine on her home desk and laptop open, Susan googled 'Toy Train Association NSW.' There was Roger's name, as the Secretary. After reading about the Association she returned to the kitchen to prepare her wild-caught salmon and decided to take her Grandmother's advice, 'Live your life so you have no regrets at the end.'

Susan sat in the third row of the meeting room. She'd arrived early for the AGM of the TTA on Saturday afternoon at the Revesby RSL dressed casually in blue jeans, white buttoned shirt and a brightly coloured rolled scarf. She intended to introduce herself to Roger so her feminine appearance was meant to impress.

A small skinny man, dressed as a train conductor prevailed on her to buy a ticket in the 'Big Train Raffle' to be drawn at the conclusion of the meeting. Susan obliged purchasing two tickets for $10.00. After all, if Roger was into toy trains then she ought to show an interest.

Roger was already sitting on the podium behind a table in

earnest conversation with an older man. 'He'd be the President' she thought. Both men were dressed conservatively, white shirt and tie and on the lapels of their jackets, the Green Loco badge. Roger was handsome, there was no doubting that, and how she admired his tidy, parted hairstyle.

The President called the meeting to order. Reports from the previous twelve months were read and questions answered. Roger's report was crisp and professional with some humorous anecdotes. His diction was perfect and he engaged the members with his eyes, unlike the president who read his report with his head down. *He has such poise and bearing* Susan thought.

Then came the election of officers. The President told the members that he was resigning after five years at the helm. Roger was voted in as the new President unopposed which didn't surprise Susan, such was his engaging demeanour and command. *A natural leader* she told herself.

No-one had nominated as Secretary. There was a pause in proceedings. Murmurings whispered through the hall. All other positions were filled by the male incumbents. The Secretarial position was left vacant and the executive was empowered to seek a suitable person.

The last item on the agenda was the drawing of the raffle. The prize was a Hornby Valley Drifter train set valued at $180.00. The Treasurer announced that the Association had made $675.00 and thanked the ticket sellers.

As a mark of respect, the outgoing President drew the ticket. He held it at a distance and theatrically called the winner's name: Susan Beveridge.

'Hello my name is Roger Milsom. Congratulations on winning the raffle. I don't believe I've met you before. Are you a member of the Association?'

'I'm intending to join, and now that I have a train set, I can play a more active role, perhaps.'

Standing face to face with Roger and in close personal proximity where she could feel his energy and heat, Susan then knew that she would become the next Secretary of the TTA of NSW.

Roger's Seduction

Roger, carrying the Hornby train set, led Susan to the car park underneath the RSL club. The boot of his red Audi S5 Coupe rose as they approached and he placed the carton inside, pulled the luggage straps taut and escorted Susan to the passenger door.

'Thank you for driving me home Roger. I don't think I could have managed on a train and bus with that heavy box.'

'Do you have a preferred way to go to Rose Bay or shall we take the cross-city tunnel?'

'It's entirely up to you. I'm happy to be driven in such a nice car.'

The interior of the sporty Audi was spotless and there was no sign of any feminine accoutrements like tissues or hand cream that might indicate a wife or girlfriend. The console was free of combs, floss and breath fresheners. Mentally she was ticking boxes.

Susan knew the vehicle was expensive but the perfect car for a man like Roger. As he concentrated on navigating the streets of Revesby, Susan examined his hands and long fingers on the black steering wheel cover. His fingernails were perfectly manicured with no hint of chewed nails, dry cuticles or cracked skin. Nor was there a wedding ring. TICK!

'I'm not exactly sure where I'll be setting up my train set. My unit is only two bedrooms.'

On the fifth floor of her apartment block she held the door open for Roger and he shuffled inside, immediately taken with the view over the harbour. It was sunset and Sydney's ferries, yachts and launches were making their way home to their moorings.

'I'd be happy to help you set it up Susan, but space will be an issue for you. Garages are the best place, I always think, because the space allows expansion. Once you get hooked with trains, it's hard not to grow your railway assets.'

'I'm going to order Thai for dinner, if you'd like to stay?'

Susan surprised herself by asking, but she wanted to reward Roger for his generosity. Before he was able to answer, she was at the fridge opening a fresh bottle of New Zealand white. She knew nothing about Roger but was entirely comfortable with him. Handing Roger a glass, she blurted,

'Is you wife jealous of your trains Roger? Does she think they take too much of your time?'

'Oh I'm not married Susan. I've had some girlfriends but they both thought I spent too much time on trains and not on them.'

They sat side by side on her deck and admired the harbour. The only interruption to their conversation was by the Uber Eats delivery. Roger, startled by the late hour of 9pm found himself quite tipsy. He'd not noticed that Susan had opened a second bottle. He grabbed the rail to steady himself.

The next morning Roger awoke to sun streaming across his naked body and the curtains wafting in the early morning north easter. His mind rewound to the delights of the previous evening.

Within months, Susan met Roger's ageing parents and was unsurprised when Roger's father told her about his 30 years as a fitter and turner at the Everleigh Railway Workshops. She was introduced to the intriguing, complex world of model trains in their double garage. She sat between Betsy and Bob while Roger explained switches, signals and solenoids. Her new Hornby set was now part of his own complex array of trains. She delighted in watching the passenger trains stop at each station, loved the clickety-clack of their little wheels and admired Roger's mastery of the remote control stick.

Within twelve months Susan became the Secretary of the TTA NSW, sold her Rose Bay unit and moved in with Roger at his Summer Hill residence. She married Roger Milsom under the big clock at Central Station and their honeymoon was a first class sleeper aboard the Trans-Siberian Railway, Moscow to Vladivostok.

Roger in Russia

Roger was in a rage. On the platform of Moscow's Leningradsky Railway Station he was remonstrating with the thick-set, middle-aged railway clerk about their allocated compartment on the Trans-Siberian train. It was not what Roger had booked, yet they were being told this inferior 'Platzkart' was their sleeper for the next 6 days.

'Platzkart is Russian sleeper.' The female official was obstinate and her ire was growing. So was Roger's frustration, expressing his displeasure with a raised voice and pointed finger. Susan was surprised and embarrassed, as she stood aside from the bickering. In the short time since they'd been together, Roger had been completely calm and in control. It surprised her that now he was aggressive and disagreeable.

They'd been in Moscow for five days, staying at the majestic Hotel Metropole near the Kremlin. Susan fell in love with the grand old building by reading the novel 'A Gentleman in

Moscow.' She was thrilled that the first week of their honeymoon would be in some of the same rooms as Count Alexander Rostov. The Count's affair with a Moscow socialite in the 1930s had so excited Susan that she acquired, at great cost, a trousseau of French lingerie for her honeymoon.

During the day Roger revelled in showing Susan the Moscow Metro, Europe's busiest underground railway system with 276 stations. They adored the extravagant interior designs of the 'Palace of the People.' In the late afternoons they strolled the parks and streets, arm-in-arm, window shopping before returning to the Metropole for dinner.

Now the 'honeymoon period' seemed to be over on the cold concrete of the platform. The Clerk stepped towards the compartment door to indicate that this was their Platzkart. She held aloft the ticket and pointed to the carriage and compartment number. Other passengers skirted silently around them making Susan feel like a delinquent.

But no, Roger was having none of it. He'd booked a sleeper, not a shared compartment where the seats became bunks, one low, one high and where strangers would be sharing the compartment.

'This is our honeymoon! How can we possibly share our bedroom? But you wouldn't know about that would you?'

Roger's sharp putdown of the stout Russian woman shocked Susan. Was this the polite Roger she knew?

'You in Russia. Speak Russian.'

The frustrated clerk excoriated Roger. She plucked a whistle from her tunic pocket and blew it shrilly three times. Two railway security guards were immediately on the spot. The uniformed Russian men towered over him, their badges shining with authority and power. Susan thought that she saw him cringe, much like his pre-loved greyhounds when he roused on them for upsetting the tracks of his toy train set. She'd accepted Roger's assertiveness and obsessiveness traits, they were not faults, but quirks of his endearing personality. This was the first time she'd seen him out of his comfort zone. The Russian authoritarianism was too much for him to bear.

'Come with us!' ordered the older security man as he clasped Roger's upper arm and roughly escorted him along the platform leaving Susan stranded, alone with their suite of honeymoon luggage.

The Clerk pivoted from Susan, ignoring her predicament and ushered an older, drably dressed couple into the shared Platz-kart compartment. Presumably, these would be the people with whom they'd spend the next five days, and nights, with a curtain between their single bunks. No wonder Roger was upset, thought Susan. And it was not what she had in mind either, wondering if it would be appropriate to be in sexy underwear whilst the couple lay in their clothes just an arms length away through the shroud.

Roger stood fuming within a drab Soviet era office of Leningradsky Station. As he checked his tickets he read 'Platzkart.' He knew enough about railway carriages to know that he didn't want to be sleeping in bunks sharing a cramped, curtained compartment with peasants. This was a dream in a lifetime. A trip on one of the World's famous railway journeys with his beautiful bride. Was this his mistake or was it Russian stand-over and gouging?

'If you want first-class sleeper then you pay an extra EURO750 plus EURO250 administration fee. We can fix quickly before train departs if you pass your credit card to me.'

This voice came from an impeccably besuited man.

This is the Workers Union henchman, stereotypical Stalin bully-boy. Iron fist in a velvet glove, Roger thought. *My E1000 will go straight to their Christmas party fund.*

When Roger was returned to Susan he was white and silent. The two security guards told them to follow. They marched toward the front of the train, the first class section. And here they found their honeymoon compartment, fit for a Tsarina, with gold trimmings, heavy velvet curtains and a bottle of chilled champagne with Beluga Black Pearl Caviar from Russia's finest Caspian sturgeons.

'Good afternoon Mr and Mrs Milsom, my name is Pavel and I am your attendant for the journey to Vladivostock. I am sorry to tell you that there is a delay in departure. If you need anything please pull on this cord, which will alert me to come to your service.'

Pavel began to reverse through the sliding door into the corridor until Roger asked, 'What is the nature of the delay? What is causing the problem?'

Roger was still agitated and annoyed at the Russian incompetence.

'Maybe I can help? After all, I am the President of the NSW Toy Train Association and I've had a lifetime of experience coordinating train movements.'

Susan saw the absurdity of Roger's posturing. She took him by the arm and urged him to sit on the side of the bed with her.

'There are many delays on Russian railways Mr Milsom. We are still plagued by old Soviet systems and attitudes. The government has not invested in rail infrastructure. Although it says 5 nights and 6 days, it can be longer.'

As Pavel was speaking, Susan admired the young man's presence. He seemed intelligent, gentle and his demeanour was pleasant, unlike the staff on the platform. He was dressed in navy pants and tight fitting jacket with red piping, perfectly crisp. Pavel seemed an archetypical railway attendant from an

Agatha Christie novel, small in stature but with masculine features, dark mysterious eyes and soft lips.

'*What a lovely name,*' Susan thought, so much nicer than Bruce or Wayne.

'What time is dinner Pavel,' she asked. 'Do we go to the dining car?'

'Dinner is at 7pm and you can choose dining room or eat here in your cabin.'

'Dining room for us please Pavel.'

Susan retorted without consulting Roger because she wanted to look at and talk to other guests. She smiled at Roger because this was the first time in their relationship she'd asserted herself in decision making. She noticed how downcast her husband looked after the altercation with the Russian railway officials.

Roger's jealousy

It was day three of the newlyweds' Russian railway honeymoon. Susan was bored witless. Roger was loving every minute and gave Susan a running commentary about the locomotive's performance, the characteristics of the carriages and the details of the Russian railway network. She pretended to listen and show interest but in realty, she was silently bemoaning her situation.

With help from Pavel, via a cash payment, Roger joined the engine drivers for an afternoon, sitting up with full view of the track and the endless expanse of sky and land. Meanwhile Susan sat alone in the cabin, staring blankly out the window at the flat, bleak tundra. She became more and more agitated. How foolish she'd been to rush into marrying this obsessive little man without even talking with him about their future together. His sole interest was trains. She was convinced he was incapable of showing any interest in her. She felt like baggage.

In her former job as a legal secretary, she'd prepared prenups for couples before entering marriage. Why hadn't she done the same for her and Roger? They'd not discussed wealth, property or money arrangements. Nor had she raised the issue of her career. Where would they live? She was not going to stay in a dark, cold semi-detached at Summer Hill next to the country's busiest railway line with two emaciated greyhounds! What about babies? Roger had never mentioned a family, and the way he was non-performing on his honeymoon, she was not expecting to get pregnant any time soon.

At the nadir of her mid-afternoon depression, there was a light rap on the door and she looked up to see Pavel, ever alert, neat and handsome.

'Would you like tea Mrs Milsom?'

Oh ... how she hated Mrs Milsom!

'Please call me Susan, Pavel, and yes, I would love tea. Where do you make it?'

'Come with me and I'll show you a Russian railway kitchen. It's functional but not very fashionable I'm afraid.'

Susan stood, stretched her long, shapely legs and followed the intriguing young man to the end of the carriage, where he unlocked a door and ushered Susan into a tiny kitchenette and storeroom. The cubicle was redolent with sandalwood from a burnt incense stick on top of the gas stove. By the window a hummock swung to and fro in cadence with the rocking of the train. Sitting on top of the bench was a samovar brewing Russian caravan tea. The floor was covered with the mellow tone of a shiraz Persian carpet. Pavel's room was functional, neat and masculine thought Susan, just like Pavel himself, and so unlike her husband.

It was intriguing for her to see his workspace and living

quarters. On a shelf at eye level she saw four matryoshka dolls, beautifully painted in different designs and colours. Pavel took one and opened the doll, revealing another identical but smaller doll inside. He handed the little wooden babushka to Susan and urged her to twist. When she completed the task there were seven dolls lined up in decreasing size, a nesting of very cute Russian tea dolls.

'This one is for you.'

Pavel passed another Matryoshka doll to Susan. He looked into her eyes as he clasped his hands around hers.

'You are a good lady.'

She saw sadness and sorrow in his black moist eyes and it twinged her emotions. They were standing close in the tiny room, eye to eye, but Pavel made no effort to move, nor did Susan. She wanted to kiss him, to thank him for the gift, to express her feelings about him as a person.

Later, sipping her tea in the cabin awaiting Roger to return, Susan reflected on her encounter with the magnetic Pavel. It was a moment in time for her when she felt an immediate attachment, a strong connection at an emotional level with a man. She had not felt this synergy with anyone else and certainly not with Roger. Her feelings towards Pavel and his situation stirred her.

'Look at this beautiful Russian doll Pavel gave to me,' she said to Roger at dinner. 'He is such a sweet and kind person. It's one of the nicest gifts I've ever received.'

Roger appeared peeved and remained silent. He sat back in his chair and drained his large glass of inky Georgian red. Susan knew he would pass out as soon as he went to bed. Some honeymoon she thought! At least she had Pavel to fantasise over.

'Be careful of the bellhop, he's just a Central Asian peasant, Susan. They are shysters, not very nice people at all.'

He spat the words across the table. Roger's contempt was

palpable. The honeymoon was not sexually enlightening, but she was being educated about his foibles, obsessions and drinking. None of these traits were attractive to her, nor did she see them before they married.

The next morning Susan left Roger reading a book on the Tsarist Romanovs and slunk down the aisle to Pavel's hideaway. The door was open and she boldly slipped inside only to find Pavel was not there. Looking around she spied a family photograph and took it in her hands, studying the two adults and four children posing outside a block of rundown units. Her heart went out to this family. She'd seen so many people in Russia living in desperately poor conditions.

The door clicked behind her and she knew it was Pavel by the sandalwood aroma of his gold courtier's jacket. The scent was distinctive, clean and seductive. She didn't turn, instead waited to feel his presence or his voice. As he reached forward around her body to take the photo his chest pressed into her back. It was not enough to push her forward, but a gentle, sustained pressure that she interpreted as deliberate and sexual. She did not resist.

'This is my family Susan. Since the photograph was taken, my father has died and now my mother looks after three teenagers in the two bedroom unit. It is hard for them. I send my wages to her for food and rent.'

Vladivostock came into view as the train wound its way down from the mountains towards the Pacific Coast. Roger urged Susan to begin packing her things. They were on a timeline to leave the train for their flight to Tokyo thence Sydney. The 'honeymoon' was over.

'I'm not returning with you Roger,' Susan said calmly. 'I'm taking the return train to Moscow with Pavel. I'm going to assist him migrate to Australia with my sponsorship.'

'What on earth do you mean Susan. You can't be serious? Don't be so silly. That Russian urchin is not worth anything to you. We've got to get back because I have a national executive meeting of the Toy Train Association on Sunday. Quickly, hurry up!'

Susan knew her actions were rash and it was not like her to base big decisions on emotion. But in the time she had spent with Pavel during the last two days, she'd learnt of his kindness, tenderness and empathy. She'd felt his strong shoulders, stroked his golden skin and explored his virile body. His passion overwhelmed her. She'd fallen in love with Pavel, and out of love with Roger.

Roger dragged his bags up the wet footpath to the front door of his house in Summer Hill. His parents and his greyhounds were waiting inside.

'Where's Susan?' his mother asked.

'Susan has found a Russian boyfriend and has deserted me.'

Roger's Rejuvenation

It had been five months since Roger returned from Vladivostock, without Susan. He'd heard nothing from his wife since her mad affair with Pavel on the Trans-Siberian Railway. The failed 'honeymoon' irked him endlessly. He was angry and worried because she had not been in contact. He fretted that his new wife had been kidnapped under the guise of Cossack love. During his worst moments he expected the terms of the ransom to be revealed at any time by her Russian captors.

When he arrived home to his bleak Summer Hill terrace, miserable greyhounds and no job, he became morose. Adding to his funk was the disillusionment that he'd not been re-elected as President of the Toy Train Association. He found it hard to accept that an elderly man from Kyneton in Victoria had won on postal votes. Roger felt completely unloved and unwanted. His mother advised that he should see a doctor because he was going through a depression.

Roger grudgingly walked his dogs twice a day, traversing the streets and parks of the inner west whilst his mind churned about the future. He was only 33 years of age and his expectations of a happily married life, a secure career and a position as head of a national organisation had been shattered. Roger wanted a fresh start to prove to himself that he wasn't a loser.

Gabriel, a part owner of the Purple Trees Cafe with his partner Terrence, had always liked Roger. They exchanged greetings most days as Gabriel prepared Roger's piccolo latte. The coffee shop suited Roger because his dogs could drink from the bowls on the footpath and the corner tables were shaded by giant jacarandas in summer. One morning Gabe served Roger's coffee and unusually, sat with him, because he knew that 'the nice man with the dogs' was doing it tough.

'What's happening Roger? You look like shit man!'

'Everything's wrong Gabe. I'm really struggling to get back into work, find some friends, start a new life.'

Gabriel and Terrence invited Roger for dinner the following night. Wine and discourse flowed freely between the three men. Terrence, older and more assertive, hated procrastination. He challenged Roger.

'If you keep doing the same thing, you'll get the same result. You gotta make changes Rog. Your whole life is ahead of you. Moping around Summer Hill with a couple of miserable dogs isn't the answer. Think big bro! It's all about downsizing these days mate. Read up on Marie Kondo, she's the guru.'

Gabe, much more helpful and empathic surprised Roger

suggesting a change of scenery.

'Why don't you move down the coast, change your situation and meet new people. We reckon you should start an Airbnb. You'd be such a good host.'

Wow, Roger wasn't thinking that big! But over time, internet research and dinners with his new mentors, he began to make serious decisions.

Roger spent the next month cataloging and photographing his train sets and supporting infrastructure. He sold his entire antique collection on e-bay to a Saudi Prince who purchased it for his son. Twelve tea chests were shipped to Riyadh. Roger now had some money in the bank.

'The dogs have to go mate, they are inhibiting your lifestyle and your future big time. They're controlling your life mate, not the other way around. Besides, what woman would want to have a relationship with a man with two high maintenance, arthritic, old greyhounds.'

It took Roger a few days for Terrence's advice to sink in. He needed Gabe's support to have them euthanised. Under the Jacaranda tree alongside Purple Trees Cafe, Gabe set up a small memorial with the dogs' names and a bunch of flowers.

The following week, taking advantage of the high real estate market, Roger sold his Terrace within three weeks of listing. Now he had serious money in the bank. He moved in with the coffee shop owners in nearby Marrickville. It was there that they began to look at opportunities not too far from Sydney, for a property suitable for Roger's temperament and potential for Airbnb.

On Sunday drives, the three explored Jervis Bay, Shoalhaven and Southern Illawarra. The bush appealed to Roger, rather than the sea, salt and sand. They met agents and visited remote properties, small acreages and bushland settings. On the drive back to Marrickville after a bistro dinner at Kiama Leagues Club, their enthusiastic chatter about possibilities, drawbacks and opportunities was energising for Roger. He allowed himself to feel excited.

After settlement and with renovation to the kitchen and guest bedroom, the elevated property overlooking Gerringong, Geroa and Seven Mile Beach was listed on the Airbnb site.

Roger's Rustic Rainforest Retreat
Jamberoo Mountain; hideaway rainforest room; tranquil setting.
Shaded verandah; ensuite; in-ground pool; lush garden.
Commune with wallabies, wombats and native birds.
Suits singles or couple seeking quiet escape; dinner on request.
$375.00 double room; $2,000.00 six nights incl. farmhouse breakfast.

Terrence and Gabriel were the first guests (pro bono). They posted a glowing review:

Roger's R R R is something we've wanted for such a long time. The quiet, beautiful setting was perfect for our relationship. The rooms are tastefully accommodated and Roger is the gorgeous, perfect host. Excellent value.
Highly recommended. *****

Roger and Renee

No-one could have predicted the devastating impact that Covid-19 would have on bookings at Roger's Rustic Rainforest Retreat Airbnb. After investing a considerable amount of money in purchasing his mountain hideaway he'd only just finalised his listing when the lockdowns commenced. Unfortunately, Roger's luxurious boutique escape was a white elephant.

As the lockdowns continued, Roger's mood plummeted and he could feel another depression coming on. In an effort to attract customers he reduced the price, much to his chagrin, worried that his hideaway might be seen as 'cheap.' He edited the marketing spiel and offered a free bottle of wine on arrival, but still nothing! He became cranky and surly because he had not been in meaningful contact with other people.

Roger's trips to town for groceries dwindled to once a week. How he hated wearing a mask! He detested using a QR code to 'sign-in.' He loathed Brad Hazzard when the Health Minister appeared on the screen to give his nightly Covid report. What a pompous prick! He was sick of hearing about the statistics, comparisons and deaths. Who cares anymore?

Roger's vivacity had completely vaporised as winter encroached. The air cooled, the morning fogs were damp and the angle of the sun's rays changed significantly such that his cottage did not warm during the day. He began to regret his decision to come to this wretched mountainside. His depression deepened. Why had so much bad luck been dumped on him?

When he searched the mirror for signs of ageing he was shocked. His face was becoming jowly, crows-feet wrinkles were evident and his eyes had lost sparkle. A paunch and love handles had made him loosen his belt a notch. He lay on the lounge in his pyjamas and dressing gown watching morning television most days lamenting his Sydney lifestyle. He missed the toy trains. If Betsy and Bob were with him he could walk them and get some exercise. There was no local coffee shop to chat with strangers. Novels could not hold his attention.

That night the distinctive ping of the Airbnb App at 11.30pm wakened him. He read the text through sleepy eyes.

*Hello Roger Milsom, you and your place look perfect for me to
escape the city and this wretched Covid thing. I am an artist
and I wish to book for four weeks. Would you have me and my
labradoodle Napoleon. Starting next Sunday please?
PS I have a very strong preference for NO MASKS?
Ms Renee Ubrihien-White*

Renee did not post a photo of herself or of her dog. It was
not mandatory, but Roger liked to be able to assess the look
of potential guests as part of his decision making to accept or
reject. He knew it was totally unethical, even illegal, to discrim-
inate based on a person's visage or somatotype. But he was very
curious.

What if Renee was disabled and she needed special care? Did
she want an evening meal each night? Will Ms Ubrihien-White
have a car and be able to get away on day trips, rather than hang
around all day? Could he handle having a female 'artiste' in his
space for a month? How old was she? And what to make of her
hyphenated name? Was it pretentious, or was it a fair dinkum
German-English aristocratic heritage?

There were so many unknowns that Roger lay awake thinking
through the ramifications of a four-week visitation. Of course, he
needed the money and the $7,000 would be paid up front. Did
he want to share a month of his life with a woman he'd not even
met? Would it be worth it? Would a lap dog be one that barked
incessantly? Perish that thought!

At 6.30am next morning with the potbelly stove warming he
replied politely to Ms Ubrihien-White despite all the queries
that had been festering for the past seven hours. The Airbnb
enquiry spurred his energy and he began to tidy, clean and pre-
pare the space

At dusk on Sunday afternoon a black BMW SUV swung boldly

into Roger's driveway. He watched through the kitchen window as Renee Ubrihien-White alighted and stretched, yoga style. There was no doubt in Roger's mind that she was expensively dressed, judging by the plush quality of the short black leather jacket and matching thigh-length shiny boots. Her hair was salt and pepper, shoulder length, with silver earrings ostentatiously dangling and jangling.

Renee was a long way from being a bohemian artist, thought Roger, more like an East Sydney Art School graduate from a Mosman stockbroking family. She walked along the path beneath Roger's rainforest trees with a relaxed swagger. It radiated poise and purpose. Clutched under her arm was a small dog of indeterminate breed.

'Hellooo...' she called loudly and shrilly, using the pitch and tone of a bush 'Cooee.'

Roger greeted her on the patio beneath the wisteria which was just beginning to flower. Neither wore a mask. Roger was well groomed himself, wearing pressed Tommy Hilfiger polo and chinos, his face cleanly shaved and nostril hairs plucked. His mood had lightened considerably knowing that he had a guest after months of gloomy anticipation.

Renee smiled warmly on approach, crunching her boots on the gravel. She offered her hand, each finger and the thumb decorated in arrays of silver rings. Long red fingernails projected toward his torso.

'Hello Roger, how wonderful to meet you in person. You're much older and shorter than your photo shows on the Airbnb site.'

Renee's opening gambit left him uncharacteristically speechless. Was her remark a put-down, a power-play or an unintentional quip? He decided to ignore it and was about to offer a warm welcome when she added,

'You'll have to be careful with this wisteria Roger. It can get away so very easily and could invade your lovely native forest in no time at all. But its lavender flowers are simply gorgeous and it will be so lovely for me to paint. I can set my easel over there outside the shed and use the cottage as the background. Just perfect.'

They stood face to face until Roger got his wits about him then began a rehearsed welcome.

'Welcome, Renee, to my Rustic Rainforest Retreat. I hope you'll enjoy your stay and be able to produce some great paintings. Let me show you the rooms and then we'll grab your bags.'

They enjoyed a pre-dinner glass of excellent Hunter Shiraz standing with their backs to the potbelly stove while Napoleon settled on his lambskin rug at her feet.

'Is the cottage to your liking Renee?'

'It's perfect Roger thank you. The kitchen is very small. It will be fine to make cups of chai but there's no way I could cook a meal there. Could I eat with you each night please?'

Although Renee seemed demanding and direct, after five hours Roger was feeling relaxed about his first guest. He considered Renee a little eccentric but was comfortable that their time together would be tolerable, if not pleasant.

Renee was a warm attractive woman and the more time they spent together the friendlier they became. At the end of the first week they slept together, their vocal sexual activity was louder than the raucous possums. Roger had never been with a woman like Renee. The three sexual partners he'd had were passive and the relationships all short lived, including his marriage with Susan. Renee, on the other hand was passionate, adventuresome and experienced.

Roger was a willing student receiving his sex education lessons daily over the next two weeks until Renee received a phone call. Her mother had taken ill in the UK and was not expected to live. She was advised to 'come home' as soon as possible. The next morning she departed telling Roger that she'd be in touch.

Roger was disappointed to say the least. He was now alone again and could feel his depressive moods returning. It was another two weeks before he had an Airbnb message.

My Dear, Dear Roger

At last I've tracked you down. I have no-one else to turn to. Pavel has been conscripted into Putin's army for the ridiculous war against Ukraine and I have been abandoned in a cold, spartan, soviet-era apartment on the outskirts of Moscow. I desperately need help to get out. I have no money or means to leave this miserable, brutal country. I can't speak the language and people here shun me because I'm a foreigner. The discrimination is very hurtful.

I have no money as Pavel and his family whittled away what savings I had. I'm sure they saw me as a rich foreigner and I now feel totally exploited. You have no idea how utterly despondent I feel about everything that has happened.

My behaviour on the Trans-Siberian Railway was atrocious and inexcusable. I am so, so, sorry for what I've done to you and to our marriage. I urgently want to make it up to you in so many ways. What a fool I've been!

Please, please help me Roger. I am desperate and I know that you still have some loving feeling for me, as I do for you. I've not stopped thinking about you since the regrettable train incident. You are such a noble, responsible and beautiful man.

I love you.
Susan

PS I am using my maiden name (Beveridge) in correspondence,
for various reasons.

Roger seeks spiritual guidance

Roger became depressive. He now found himself in the worst possible circumstances. At the urgings of his Sydney friends, he purchased return air fares Sydney to Townsville so he could thaw out and take further stock of his life. He'd booked five days at Pepper's on Magnetic Island intending to swim, bush walk and recommence his meditation sessions. The first morning on the island he was on the bus to Horseshoe Bay.

Roger strolled through the stalls at the Sunday morning markets admiring the hand-made jewellery, artist seascapes and island bric-a-brac. Nothing persuaded Roger to purchase a memento but he did buy a mango smoothy. The thick sweet dairy mix refreshed him, especially the ice-cream scoops stranded in the bottom of the plastic container.

He glanced at a curious sign advertising 'Channelled Readings.' The foolscap notice leant against a small tent nestled under whispering casuarinas. A worn piece of red and indigo Persian carpet covered the coarse sand and small casuarina nuts. It seemed a perfect site for psychic exploration on this warm morning. Peeking in her saw two women sitting at a card table. Two chunks of crystal weighed stacks of cards as insurance against the growing sea breeze. Without wanting to be conspicuous he caught the eye of the woman facing the doorway. She glanced up and smiled warmly. Roger moved on smartly, not wanting to be engaged even though his curiosity was aroused.

Roger pondered what 'Channelled Readings' meant, so he turned back, determined to ask. Psychics, tarot cards and soothsayers were familiar words, but he had never considered entering the spiritual realm. He did not want to spend $25 for fifteen minutes but he was sure the friendly lady would appraise him briefly about the readings.

The camping chair for clients was unoccupied. The 'moderator' smiled and observed the man in the doorway. Around 40 years old she guessed, reasonably healthy and fit although she did notice the development of man boobs and some love handles bulging his tight-fitting royal blue Tommy Hilfiger polo. She also noticed two deep creases between his eyebrows that puckered his forehead and the grey tinges in his hair.

Roger found himself unwittingly sitting deeply in the camping chair. It was as if he'd been unconsciously pulled into the tent by a mysterious force. He clenched his buttocks to stand, but the chair gripped him in a comfortable embrace. He only wanted to ask a simple question.

'Hello I'm Kayla,' she said. 'And who are you?'

Her welcoming relaxed tone pleased Roger. He felt very comfortable in her presence even though he'd been there for only thirty seconds.

'I'm Roger. I just wanted to know what Channelled Readings meant.'

'This is where we explore your spirit world.'

'Is it fortune telling?' enquired Roger.

Kayla's lustrous chocolate-coloured hair spilled over her shoulders and down her back. Her black-rimmed, rectangular spectacles highlighted dark arched eyebrows. A single gold ring pierced her left nostril and perfect white teeth were framed by soft pink lips. Her skin was flawless. Roger tried not to stare. His eyes travelled downwards to the thick leather cord hanging around her neck. In the neckline of her low cut broderie anglaise blouse, nestled a large crystal pendant.

'Let's have a look at some of these cards.' Kayla began to shuffle a deck of oversized well-worn cards. 'That'll give us some insight into your life and then we can dig a bit deeper with the other pack.'

Kayla asked Roger to shuffle and place the deck in the middle of the table. She took nine cards and placed them face up in a three-by-three pattern. Roger noticed the writing on some of the cards – Ten of Pentacles, The Hermit, The Devil, Seven of Cups, Page of Wands, Seven of Swords.

Kayla studied the arrangement. She nodded and smiled without speaking to Roger. She then produced a crystal on a silver lead and held it above the cards. The crystal began to twirl in a clockwise direction.

'Your life until now has been strained, hasn't it Roger? I can see there have been some stress points at times. You are not well off financially, but that's going to change. You've been wandering for a while with no permanent roots or attachments.'

Kayla paid intense attention to Roger's non-verbal reaction, searching his eyes and face for signs of any discomfort or hints of joy. He was aware that the crease lines between his eyebrows deepened when he was stressed. He was determined not to give away any information to the attractive female soothsayer wishing her to do all the predicting from the tarot cards.

'But Roger, you have a very interesting and satisfying life ahead. You're about to go through a major transition. I can see from these cards that you're going to do more travelling.'

There was silence for a minute as Kayla concentrated on the cards.

'Your need for structure and organisation in your life will soon be met by a new interest in a fascinating hobby. It will replace the childhood fascination you had with trains.'

Roger was aghast. *How could she possibly know about his train interest?* His eyes widened and mouth opened. Kayla stared intently at Roger. She reached for the crystal and it swung over the cards.

'As part of the transition I am seeing a positive development in romance, not immediately but within the foreseeable future. It will be a turbulent relationship initially before maturing into long term affection and respect.'

Kayla closed her eyes again. Roger studied her. Was she communicating with the spirit world? Her accuracy had astonished him. When she suddenly opened her eyes, he felt a flush spread across his face.

'My aboriginal father told me many wise things Roger. In life, when you leave a dark room, you'll go into light. There will always be a future and that is where we should be focussing. Your spiritual aura is bright. There is a lot of light in front of you.'

'How long have you been doing this Kayla?' Roger asked. 'Do you live on the island?'

'I'm here every week if you want to come and see me next Sunday. Unfortunately we'll have to finish now. I have some other people who've made appointments. I do hope things work out for you. The spirit realm has lots of positive energy for you.'

Kayla smiled as she pushed the Square payment reader towards him.

'It's $25 for the fifteen minutes please.'

Roger extracted himself from the camp chair, tapped his card and offered his hand to Kayla.

'Thank you for the insight Kayla. It's been enlightening for me. I'm pleased to have found you.'

Kayla's hand was warm, soft and firm. She smiled and pushed her business card across the table. During his lunch of fish and chips at the pub across the road, he studied the business card 'Guided by Spirit.' The front side was adorned in aboriginal art, of meeting places and the dreamtime spirits. The reverse, a mandala was entitled 'Unlimited Potential With Love.'

Kayla's email address was provided. Roger slipped it into his wallet as he considered what his channelled readings meant.

Roger finds peace

Upon return from the North Queensland odyssey to his rainforest retreat on the South Coast, Roger began to search for work. All Covid restrictions had been lifted so he opened his home again for Airbnb bookings. At least this would provide some income while he searched for a 'proper job.' Rather than seek for work online, Roger decided that he would use an employment agency because he knew his presence and personality would prevail compared with an impersonal paper resume.

At Select Global in Bowral he met with Mrs Brenda Southwell, one of the firm's principals. Roger was impressed with her immaculate make up, expensive string of pearls and smart navy suit. He'd worn his dark Italian suit with blue tie because he knew the Southern Highlands was staunchly liberal. Mrs Southwell, he thought, may have connections to the party even though Roger, of working class origins from Summer Hill, had always voted Labor. However, in the last elections he'd supported the Teals in the Senate.

Late that evening while climbing into his crisp one-thousand thread count bed sheets and David Alexander Shetland Doona he heard the distinctive Airbnb App ping. It was a request for four days from Elizabeth Wishart-Snape. Roger was pleased to have a client and he accepted immediately because he needed the money.

Roger was preparing the room for the new guest the next day when his phone rang. It was a secretary from Select Global asking if Roger could come into their office to meet Mrs Southwell to discuss 'an opportunity.' He was surprised and pleased that something had come up so quickly. Maybe a new career to herald a more successful life into the future.

Mrs Southwell, 'please call me Beverly,' greeted Roger and took him to her office where she sat behind her desk.

'Roger, I have a job which I think suits you. We've washed your profile across our database of vacancies and believe we have a very good match. Your personality is such that you find it easy to talk with people and to engage with them at a meaningful level. This is a role that you can do from home in your own time, which would mean no travel, except for occasional training at the Head Office in Sydney.'

Beverly paused then continued.

'The job is telephone sales with Thistlethwaite Wines, one of Australia's best boutique wine sellers. Their clients are mostly affluent, middle to older age who consider themselves to be wine connoisseurs. The role is to grow the database and to increase volume and value from their existing customers. We think you are an outstanding applicant and it's a job that you can make your own for many years to come. Potentially, you can do very well out of this financially.'

Roger considered the role carefully on his drive home down the escarpment. He decided that he had nothing to lose by accepting. He rang Beverley the next morning to confirm. She was delighted.

'I hope we can stay in touch Roger. I'd love to come and look at your Rainforest Retreat. It sounds like a lovely place for a weekend break. I'll give you a ring in a few weeks time to see how the job is going. Good luck.'

In no time at all Roger was at Thistlethwaites in Woolloolo-moo for five days of training, including two days where he began ringing clients while an experienced wine marketer sat beside him and listened in on Roger's telephone skills. He still struggled with the pronunciation of Thistlethwaites, finding it a real tongue twister.

'Hello Mary, this is Roger from Thistlethwaite Wines calling, how are you today?'

'Hello, who is it?'

'I'm ringing to see if you'd like to order any champagne. We have a special on at the moment and it's coming up to Christmas.'

'You're not the normal chap who rings! What's happened to him?'

'He is working elsewhere I believe. I've taken his place and I'm looking forward to getting to know you a little better, especially your wine preferences.'

Roger looked at Mary's past purchases on the database.

'Oh, and Mary, we have some nice Pinot Noir from France. It's very soft with lovely truffle tones. I could put a bottle or two in with your champagne for you to try if you'd like.'

'That does sound nice. What did you say your name was?'

The training was highly successful according to his trainer and Roger returned home determined to get to know his clients and sell them more and more wine. He enjoyed these 'wine friends' and made sure the essence of every conversation was recorded so he could develop an on-going dialogue. One of his favourites was Major General Hugh Bellingham (Retired) who loved 'big reds.' His orders of Shiraz, Cabernet Sauvignon and Argentinian Malbec were in the dozens each month. It was worthwhile for Roger to listen to the Major General tell his war stories from Iran and Afghanistan.

Roger loved the work because he learnt the best time to ring was late afternoon so that gave him mornings free.

Elizabeth Wishart-Snape was due to arrive for her four day Airbnb stay. He had no details of her, not even a photo. Roger cleaned the guest bedroom and bathroom and ensured the room was well aired. There was nothing better than the fresh cool scents of the rainforest filling the room. A small Hyundai pulled up on the driveway and a familiar figure walked towards the house.

'Hello Roger. It's so nice to see you.'

Susan, Roger's wife who betrayed him on the Trans-Siberian Railway stood in front of him. He was speechless. How and why was she here? Has she used a pseudonym to trick me?

'I found you on the Airbnb site. It's such a lovely photo of you. I do hope you won't be cranky about me staying here. I am looking forward to chatting with you about our lives since that wretched honeymoon. How long has it been now, three years?'

Susan stayed on, and on, and on, taking over the management of Roger's Rainforest Retreat Airbnb. Because they had not divorced they resumed life as a married couple. Together they developed an interest in Lego and converted their double garage into a Lego Land. They are proud parents of a young Irish Setter named Sinead. They plan to become breeders with her.

Roger continues to build Thisthlethwaites' business through his very congenial phone manner. He was awarded the 'Outstanding Salesman of the Year in 2021-2022.'

Beverley Southwell convinced Roger to join the local branch of the Liberal Party. He is considering standing for preselection for the seat of Gilmore in the Federal Parliament.

The Commandant's Bath

Major James Morisset
Commandant and Magistrate
Newcastle Penal Settlement, NSW,
February 1819

Dear beloved Mother,

I trust this letter finds you in good health and high spirits after your long winter. Are your favourite jonquils already blooming in London? You'll be very proud to learn that Governor Macquarie has upgraded my rank to Major, as well as to the Commandant's posting at Newcastle. I now have oversight of 650 convicts, many of them rough heads from Ireland and recalcitrant absconders. I have the respect of my regiment of 88 marines and enjoy the challenge of being a Penal Administrator.

The summer here has been stifling, as there is a touch of the tropics on this coast. Fortunately, I've found a delightful place to cool off in the fresh salty water. We noticed some of the native boys jumping into a 'Bogey Hole,' a pool on a rock shelf that is constantly replenished by the ocean swell. It is quite small, so I've formed a work gang of six convicts to enlarge it. It's known among the settlement that I like to bathe in the sea, hence they are calling it the Commandant's Bath. I believe it is the first pool to be constructed in the Colony.

I swim there most days at dawn so I can watch the brilliant orange sun rise out of the vast Pacific. I share this indulgence with small striped fish, octopus and busy little crabs that constantly scuttle between rock crevices. On a calm morning I await a pod of dolphins to inspect me, just as I review the regiment – eye to eye! Babies cruise beside their mothers as the family glides ever so close. They are such a delight. I'm told that we shall soon see whales travelling north. Gulls and sometimes a sea eagle lift and swoop in the updrafts of the tall cliffs above. They are nothing like Dover's White Cliffs but the blue Pacific is so inviting compared to the muddy English Channel.

When the sea is rough it's unsafe to bathe in the 'Bogey Hole.' The waves break heavily on the rocks and throw enormous spumes up the cliffs; then the water cascades back down to cover the pool in a sparkling white blanket. The thud of the waves reminds me of those dreaded explosions of artillery in that infernal war in Spain. The thump still causes me to gird my loins! You'll be pleased to know that the cleansing cold water makes my skin tingle and has done wonders for the shrapnel scar on my cheek. The redness has subsided and I'm told by the doctor that it no longer looks angry. So my youthful good looks are being restored, dear Mother, thanks to the healing powers of my pool!

I shall write again soon from the Antipodes. I am so far away from you, but you are always close in my heart. I have the honour to be your loving son,

JAMES

Ice Cream

Within my village, a new shop opened recently. When I read the signage proclaiming 'Smiths Ice Cream,' I was intrigued because I'd never thought that successful ice cream retailing could be achieved with a common surname like Smith. Somehow 'Smiths' has always gone with salty, crunchy chips, but not ice cream. On the other hand, we have 'common' names like Peters, Paul's and Streets ice cream, so why not Smiths?

I love ice cream. My favourite has always been vanilla. Nowadays, it's labelled 'vanilla bean.' There's a sapidity about Smithy's vanilla bean that I've not experienced since my first taste of ice cream 69 years ago. I've been hooked on the cold, sweet, melting elixir ever since. In the town where I grew up, corner shops sold ice cream in sallow wafer cones. Sugar or waffle cones came later. I graduated to double cones as soon as my budget allowed.

My first attempt to lick a cone without a helping hand was a disaster. The ice-cream toppled off onto the pavement. I was totally overcome with grief. Since that early mishap, I quickly learnt that as soon as you accept a cone, be sure to press the cold frozen cream downwards with the lips to ensure it sits firmly.

Back in the day when electrification enabled households to purchase white goods, my Auntie Pat was one of the first in town to retire her 'Silent Knight' kerosene fridge. Her new Westinghouse had a small inner cubicle that produced ice blocks and in which new frozen food products like peas, corn and ice cream could be stored.

At one family Sunday lunch Auntie Pat surprised us with a Neapolitan Brick for dessert, to be shared among 8 people. I was in awe of this pink, white and chocolate ice-cream rectangle, amazed that the plastic cardboard could be peeled away to reveal such manna. After older cousins and siblings helped themselves, there was a melting mess left for me. I've been making up for the loss ever since.

Australians are the third biggest consumers of ice cream behind the US and NZ. It's not surprising given our climate and the bewildering array of ice confections. Ted and Daisy Street began their ice cream business at Corrimal in 1930 and went on to develop the Paddle Pop, the biggest selling per capita ice cream unit in the history of the world. My contribution to the record came with hundreds of purchases of caramel paddle pops from the school canteen. Streets went on to bigger and better things such as the complex Golden Gaytime, the Italianate Cornetto (far superior to Peter's Drumstick) and the formidable double-dipped Belgian chocolate Magnum.

I discovered Affogato a decade or two ago; expresso coffee with vanilla ice cream. Good coffee houses will serve the black nectar and the ice cream in separate bowls or glasses. I like to pour the coffee in small amounts over the top of the ice cream, then sip the resultant sweetened, creamed liquid. Repeat until all products are consumed.

In our travels across the globe I've always tried to taste the local ice cream. The United States had Dairy Queen soft serve. 'Scrump-deli- icious dairy queen' went the jingle. I always chose their banana split served in a long, boat-shaped bowl, with chocolate sauce and sprinkled with nuts. Every month the University campus Dairy Queen held a 'Specials Night' – purchase one banana split for 99 cents, buy another for 1 cent. Guess what? The queue went for two blocks. It was worth the wait on a hot summer night, taking a break from studies.

Most weeks I have a tub of Connoisseur Vanilla in the freezer. It's often on special at the local IGA. But now that Smithy has proper ice cream just down the road, I'll be bringing five substantial scoops of Jersey milk ice cream home in a Styrofoam pack. It's only $3.00 a scoop. What a bargain!

Cycling Home

Home is a backyard of space, sky, sunlight with
grey paling fences and towering eucalypts shadowing rusty roofs.
I plant vegetables, pluck nectarines and collect warm eggs,
play matchbox toys in driveway dirt with imaginary friends and
shiver from a sprinkler on fresh cut lawn.

Home is a neighbourhood of streets, paddocks and tracks
explored on a hand-me-down bike with back-pedal brakes.
I race flotsam boats in flooded gutters,
wallow in warm river shallows and
dream below the casuarina susurrus.

Home is a beach of warm sand, ripples and
the exhilaration of body surfing.
I sun bake with zinc-creamed nose and coconut oiled body
next to a Melbourne girl in a bikini as
Buddy Holly sings from surf club loud speakers.

Home is unhinged as the city entices. I break comfortable bonds
with trepidation, excitement and expectation.
I flit between ateliers, share houses and flats,
suffer hangovers, pub food, blow budgets and
drift, lonely, morose and confused.

Home is a loving partner who
provides intimacy, companionship and clarity.
We secure jobs, an old house, a damaged Datsun.
Home has a backyard of space, sunlight and a blonde haired
    baby boy.

Home is family, neighbours and friends with
discovery through travel, books and creativity.
We nurture each other into comfortable older age.
I plant vegetables, pluck nectarines and collect warm eggs
beneath towering eucalypts shadowing rusty roofs.

Alexei's Love Story

Alexei was surprised that he would have to pay to use the toilet. When he turned to look at the woman with the officious voice he saw her head and shoulders above the highly polished counter. She was impeccably neat and tidy and her brunette hair was pulled tight into a bun. Around her neck was a silk scarf with cerise splashes that matched her lipstick.

'Two hundred roubles please,' she demanded.

'But I work here in the mall.' Alexei appealed.

'It makes no difference, everyone has to pay – it's the regulations.'

Annoyed at her intransigence, but unable to hold his bladder, Alexei quickly placed two coins on the counter and hurried inside to do his business. As he stood at the wide, deep urinal, with wooden panels each side for privacy, he smelt the strong odour of bleach and admired the cleanliness and spaciousness of the impressive bathroom. Alexi wondered about the woman attendant whom he expected to be an older, dour woman with starched uniform. She was anything but, appearing as an attractive brunette, mid-forties and nicely rounded. Her face was welcoming and she wore makeup, a little unusual for a Russian woman working in a job like this.

'By the way,' she said as Alexei came out of the men's room. 'Here is your receipt.'

She emerged from behind the counter, stood in front of him and offered the slip of paper. As he took it he replied:

'I am Alexei Tulsky and I am the new security officer at Coffee

Mania on the second level.'

'Oh then,' she said more brightly, smiling at Alexei. 'You can ask the Coffee Mania people to give you a voucher so that you don't have to pay. But I can't let you in for free because the Historic Toilet has its own budget and targets to meet, just like other businesses in the mall. I am accountable for all transactions here. My name is Svetlana.'

The vanilla bean fragrance wafting from Svetlana was pleasantly welcome after the disinfectant of the urinals. The aroma softened her persona and now that she was closer to him he noticed the red, tear-shaped ear rings that matched the colour of her lips and scarf. She was far from being a stern, frumpy, stereotypical Russian woman.

Alexei considered the merits of applying a capitalist business model to the workings of a bathroom. It confirmed for him that the western system was idiotic. There were some things from the soviet era that should be retained, he silently fumed, especially free public lavatories but he knew that Russia would never return to bolshevism. Now, it was everybody for themselves and forget about the collective. As he ascended the wide staircase from lower level 1 up to the ground floor he noticed the sepia photographs of Tsars, Tsarinas and celebrities who had used the facility. Even Lenin and his entourage featured in the exhibition.

Alexei returned to the coffee shop to begin his afternoon shift and approached his supervisor.

'What is the Historic Toilet and may I have a voucher to use it please?'

'Of course,' she said. 'Isn't it beautiful? It's a renovated bathroom from Nicholas III time. He was a conservative Tsar and wanted the upper classes to follow his dictums and present the absolute best to the Russian people and to the world. So this bathroom was built with Italian marble and French oak. The faucets were gold plated. There were showers so gentlemen could look their best when meeting with government officials or other businessmen. This was in pre-revolutionary times and, as you know, Lenin and Stalin spurned everything to do with the Royal family, so the toilets were left to pilfering and neglect. We're all so pleased that the new owners have restored the bathroom to its majestic state. It's quite an attraction for visitors don't you think? And that brings us more customers, so it's a good thing.'

◆

As part of his orientation for the job, Alexei attended a one-day induction class along with five other new security recruits. He learnt that Coffee Mania Inc was a franchise, a term that was new to him, and that the owner was the son of a rich oligarch. He was not surprised by this fact and admitted privately to himself that working for an oligarch and his family was no different to being a part of the privileged people who 'worked' for the Tsars.

The young instructor read from the handout. She emphasised that the restaurant chain must present a 'contemporary dining experience for clients.' Above all else, customer service and satisfaction is a 'primary and fundamental outcome.' She then asked the men to 'workshop' how they, in their security roles could help ensure 'customer satisfaction for each and every one of our clients.'

Alexei felt that this exercise failed to elicit the responses that were expected. He was not expected to speak to clients, he was there to ensure safety and order, prevent theft and apprehend clients and staff who acted outside the Coffee Mania 'Behavioural Protocol.'

After a lunch break the inductees were introduced to the Business Manager – Food Procurement and Preparation. The slim young man, dressed in a tight blue suit with open-necked, white shirt sat on the edge of the table in front of them and explained the company's philosophy of sourcing products.

'Customers,' he said, 'need to know that our products are ecologically sustainable, especially our teas and coffee beans that are organically grown and from single origin sources.'

The trainees were handed a folder with colour-coded sheets explaining Coffee Mania's mission and expected business outcomes over a five year period. A PowerPoint presentation illustrated the company's operations, reporting, staffing and business partners. Alexei's head was spinning.

At the end of the day, he was told that he'd been appointed to Coffee Mania's restaurant in Moscow's revamped, upmarket GUM Shopping Mall. It was, in the words of the trainer, their 'newest, biggest and most prestigious restaurant.' The cavernous, newly renovated department store, bordering the western edge of Red Square accommodated some of the world's most expensive brands such as Bulgari, Swatch, Boss, Apple, Intimissimi, Prada and Monolo Blahnik. These names meant nothing to Alexei who was still in shock, knowing that he had been selected for the number one cafe.

During the 40 minute trip on the Metro, returning to his cold apartment, Alexei felt like he had achieved a sense of inclusion and connection with the company. He was proud of his first job in this new economic system adopted since Perestroika, even though he didn't understand it.

Alexei arrived at work on his first day at 7.30am for orientation.

'A feature of the restaurant is our pastries, cakes and cookies,' the supervisor told Alexei.

'When customers choose a baked delight to go with their soy latte or chai they often snap a selfie to add to their facebook or instagram page. Our social media presence is so important for the business.'

Alexei nodded without understanding.

'Please sit here to sample a drink and a cake of your choice as part of our welcome to you, Alexei.'

The supervisor smiled as she indicated a table in the corner.

'White coffee and chocolate chip biscuit please,' Alexei responded to the waitress after he had perused the 12-page, illustrated laminated menu.

At the end of his workday, Alexei was pleased that he had secured the job with the Coffee Mania franchise in the new shopping mall. He felt 'modern' in this restaurant. The expensive coffee brews, herbal teas, pastries, and cakes were strange to him, but they obviously appealed to the clientele, who, Alexei assumed, were the daughters and wives of rich Russian men.

◈

'Good afternoon Mr Tulsky,' a smiling Svetlana greeted Alexei as he passed the voucher to her at the beginning of his lunch break.

'Is your new job in the coffee shop going well for you?'

'Yes, it is. I'm finding it to my liking thank you. And what about you Svetlana, how long have you been working here?'

'Two years now, ever since it opened Mr Tulsky. I really, really enjoy it and I love chatting to all the different people who come down to look and use the historic facility. It attracts many tourists from all over the world you know.'

As she spoke she appraised the short, solid man with a paunch. He was well presented and clean-shaven, pressed canary yellow shirt, maroon tie, dark trousers and polished shoes. Possibly early fifties, although it was always hard to know with Russian men, she pondered. Of most interest to her were his dark eyes set in a pleasant and kindly face. It will be nice to have him as one of my regulars she thought to herself.

'Please call me Alexei, Svetlana. Being comrades in the same establishment warrants a first name understanding, don't you think?'

'What a beautiful name, it really suits you. My uncle's name was Alexei and he was a really handsome and generous man. He died only five years ago.'

'I'm sorry to hear that. Now I must go for my lunch and get back to work. The lunch breaks are short here. Its quite different to the old days when they really looked after the workers.'

At the end of his second week, Svetlana entered the cafe during her morning tea break. She smiled at Alexei, who was surprised to see her. She took a seat where she could watch him. While sipping her mug of cappuccino she noticed Alexei standing over the selections in the cake cabinet. Immediately she rose and walked across.

'Which ones do you like the best Alexei?' she asked him.

Without speaking he pointed to the torte, an extravagant layered cream, fruit and chocolate cake.

'Oh! I love chocolate too,' she smiled and proceeded to order.

Without speaking he shook his head and pointed. A waitress appeared and Svetlana returned to her table to await the torte to be delivered according to Coffee Mania protocol.

As she savoured the cake, dabbing the cream from her lips with a paper serviette, she appraised Alexei as he went about his security routine. He did not wear a wedding ring, nor any other jewellery. There were no broken capillaries on his face, which was often a telltale sign of excessive vodka drinking in Russian

men. His white teeth indicated that he didn't smoke and impor-
tantly for her, he had those engaging dark eyes with long lashes.
His ancestors were surely from the Caucasus with eyes like that,
she mused. All those features were very appealing.

Just as Svetlana was finishing, a horde of Asian tourists
flooded into the plush chairs and lounges of the restaurant
Alexei took refuge behind one of the gothic styled columns. He
was caught off guard, not expecting so many people all at once.
How could he exercise surveillance?

Svetlana, too, was surprised especially by their noisy chatter
and their excited jostling over the cake cabinet. She looked for
Alexei and saw him standing firmly by the cakes in the midst of a
dozen elderly Chinese people.

It was then that she noticed his head twitch, ever so slightly.

◆

Uncharacteristically for a Russian woman, Svetlana was some-
times coquettish with men. If she liked the look of a man she
was want to start a conversation with him. And so it was with
Alexei.

On his afternoon visits to the Historic Toilet, when he turned
at the bottom of the steps, Svetlana emerged from behind the
high counter to engage him. She stood facing him, left hand on
her thigh, fingers spread and her right arm on her hip in her His-
toric Toilet uniform of black skirt, stockings and high-heeled
shoes. The fitted blouse strained across her chest emphasising
a full bosom and showing a tiny glimpse of her bra. On the left
side, high on her chest was her identification tag.

GUM INC MALL
Historic Toilet
Svetlana Chabanov
Empl# C305476 9

Alexei began to linger and chat to Svetlana. He liked the look of her and he liked her conversational style. She seemed to put him at ease, and he liked that. In previous relationships he'd found his female friends too bossy, cool and judgemental. They were quick to temper and consequently the friendships failed because he found it too stressful. Svetlana's warm demeanour was welcoming and she looked directly at his face and into his eyes which he found unnerving because no other woman had ever shown such intensity.

As the weeks went by, they learnt more about each other sharing their childhood stories, interests and living arrangements. Svetlana volunteered more personal information than Alexei.

'I was married at 22 yrs and it ended after three years,' she confided offhandedly one day.

'I've had had some boyfriends since then but none of the relationships flourished. It's hard to find a good man these days. Most of them drink too much, they're lazy and only talk about themselves.'

Alexei noted the things she disliked, secretly self-rating his opportunity for a friendship.

'What about you Alexei?' She asked, probing to discover more of his background.

'I was sent to the armed conflict in the Chechnyan Republic in 1995 after my first year of military conscription. I was 19 years.' Alexei's head began to twitch slightly.

'I was wounded with schrapnel in the shoulder and neck.

I am fully recovered but the doctors told me that I have some neurological damage. I took a long time to recover through rehabilitation.'

His head twitch was more marked now. 'As a result, I have had very limited opportunities to form relationships with any other person, especially a woman.'

Svetlana nodded sympathetically, looked into his eyes and silently urged him to reveal more.

'The Army helped me get my life in regular order and to settle back into society. I have a modest pension and I live with another veteran in an apartment near Domodedovo airport.'

His head twitch had eased, as if he were relieved to have things off his chest. He straightened up, looked at his watch and began to move away.

'I must go now, I don't want to be late.'

He turned and quickly strode up the steps two by two, back to his place of employ.

Svetlana was left standing on the marble, her heart aching for this man she'd recently met.

◈

Alexei did not return to the Historic Toilet for the next two days. But on Friday Alexei descended the steps with a plate covered by a table napkin and offered it to Svetlana. Alexei opened his hands and motioned for her to reveal the gift. She put her hands to her cheeks and looked at Alexei who was smiling back at her. Spontaneously Svetlana ran to Alexei and embraced him. It was a close and lingering hug.

'It's my favourite chocolate torte, thank you Alexei.'

Alexei became so smitten by Svetlana that he began to bring a slice of pilfered cake from the Coffee Mania cabinet on days when the cakes were not selling well. Svetlana rewarded him with a hug and sometimes with a kiss.

However Alexei's thieving came to the attention of a waitress who saw him remove the torte and smuggle it away at the lunch break. She knew that this was forbidden and went straight to the supervisor. Upon his return he was summoned to the office.

'Alexei, have you been taking cakes from the cabinet without paying?'

He remained silent, shocked about the directness of the question and alarmed that he'd been detected. His head began to twitch.

'I have evidence of you stealing, Alexei.' She showed a photograph on her phone of him presenting the cake to Svetlana.

'Do you have anything to say?' said the inquisitor.

Silence prevailed.

'Alexei, you are still in your three month trial period and whilst we were happy with your progress we cannot have a thief in our company. I am personally very disappointed because we all liked you. I'm sorry, but your employment is terminated. You will be paid to the end of this week.'

Alexei was distraught. He couldn't speak. He was rooted to the spot with his head twitching uncontrollably.

'Thank you, you may go now, please leave the building.'

He quickly made his way down to Svetlana.

◆

Svetlana took Alexei by the arm and led him onto the street, hailed a taxi and drove to the apartment that she shared with her 75-yr-old mother. Once inside, she served tea and calmed Alexei's agitated state.

'Everything will be all right,' she said repeatedly, nursing his hand.

Her mother, Olga came into the room with a scented candle and placed it next to Alexei.

He nodded at the older woman in appreciation and as the fragrant rosemary permeated the room Alexei began to settle.

'Mother is a big believer in the power of herbs,' said Svetlana. 'Her church group share stories of their childhood growing up on the collective farms and how they collected herbs to use in cooking and medicines. She loves the candles we buy every month at the markets. There is never a day goes by without a scented candle burning in our apartment. Their scent is so calming for the soul.'

Alexei managed a wan smile at Olga. Svetlana noticed that his twitch had eased.

'And the tea is from Turkestan. It has wonderful relaxing properties. I'm sure you can taste the camomile and the valerian root. It will help you to relax.'

Alexei looked at the ancient samovar sitting on the sideboard and wondered how many cups of tea it had dispensed. As the afternoon waned, Alexei, feeling stronger, stood and announced:

'I must go now. It's getting late. Thank you for your hospitality.'

Svetlana jumped to her feet.

'You are not going anywhere in that state Alexei Tulsky. Come with me.'

She took him by the hand and led him to the bathroom where she ran a hot bath. Her mother followed with a bottle of vanilla oil. The women persuaded Alexei to undress and get in.

'Please use the soap and the shampoo.'

He did as he was told after they had bundled up his clothes and left the room, door ajar. The warm water was soothing for him, the vanilla fumes intoxicating and he lay back to consider his situation.

'Alexei, I'm going out for twenty minutes. Please stay in the bath until I return.' Svetlana announced through the crack in the door.

He lay back to enjoy the warm water topping it up twice before Svetlana returned.

'Here is some new underwear for you and a dressing gown. Your others were filthy and mother is washing them. Now, please get out and I will dry you off.'

Svetlana raised the towel in front of her face, shielding her eyes. Alexei did as he was told, not knowing what he should do or say. Gently she put the towel around his waist, looked into his eyes and kissed him. He pulled on his new white singlet and red polka dot boxer shorts.

It was dark now and the apartment was full of cooking aromas. Alexei came into the kitchen in his byzantine blue dressing gown. Fragrant chicken, bay leaves, paprika, potatoes and cabbage made him suddenly hungry. At the table, Svetlana poured vodka and proposed:

'Nostrovia!'

The three dined together, Alexei looking like a new man.

'It's best for you to stay here tonight Alexei. You're too upset to go all that way back to your cold apartment. We are going to watch the movie 'Ekaterina' on television tonight.'

Alexei was silent, as if obeying orders from his sergeant after five years in the army. They watched the movie on her old leather lounge. Svetlana then ushered him to her bedroom, undid the dressing gown, turned back the sheets on her double bed. Olga peeped around the corner of the door.

Alexei had never lay in a woman's bed before. Anxious and confused with his head twitching markedly, he thought about his sacking and his new situation of being unemployed. Today's events had happened so fast. He had never conceived he would be in this situation and he felt the guilt of theft burn into his soul.

Svetlana returned from the bathroom in a black negligee and slinked between the sheets beside him. They lay looking at each other in the soft yellow light of the bedside lamp.

'I'll take care of you Alexei, you are a good man.' She cupped his face in her hands to steady his head.

She kissed him again, rolled over to turn off the light, then cuddled up to him. Under the sheets Svetlana gently seduced him, despite his protesting head. At denouement, Alexei was perfectly calm, not one tic. He looked like a little boy. They both slept soundly.

◆

Alexei stayed on with Svetlana and her mother. During the day when Svetlana went to work, he and Olga enjoyed daily chess contests listening to Rimsky-Korsakov, Stravinsky and other Russian composers. Alexei became quite attached and thankful towards Olga. She made him borscht, his favourite food and they chatted about the Soviet days. Over time, as he became more comfortable and accepting, his head twitching disappeared.

Svetlana took him shopping and bought modern clothes and shoes so he'd look less like a security guard and more like a handsome middle aged man. They went to a corner bar down the road where Svetlana proudly introduced him to two of her friends. Alexei sipped some Georgian red wine and began to relax, joining in the conversation and laughing at their jokes. After gossiping and giggling, the three women went off to the bathroom leaving Alexei alone at the small table.

'Svetlana, I love the look of your new man. Can you get one

for me?' asked one friend.

'You're so lucky Lana, you better make sure you look after him well, give him everything he needs, you know what I mean,' the other friend said giggling.

Towards the end of summer, Svetlana returned from work very excited.

'I've found you a new job Alexei. It's just the one for you! One of my clients at the Historic Toilet is the owner of a sweet factory and they want a man to work in the packing and dispatch section with three others. I told him that I have the perfect man for the job,' she giggled as she cupped his face.

Svetlana accompanied Alexei to the factory quite close to the beautiful Komsomolskaya Metro Station. When they left, Alexei was newly employed and would begin work the following Monday.

At the end of the first week, he came home with a gift for Svetlana and Olga. It was a paper bag of mixed sweets.

'Oh Alexei, you haven't stolen it, have you?'

Alexei smiled and shook his head.

'All the factory employees are given one bag of sweets each week to take home. Being at work is like being in one big happy family.'

Svetlana and Olga embraced him. Tears stung his eyes.

Skinny Dip

I love to swim in the seas of Australia and
here on the Freycinet in southern Tasmania
it's dawn in spring and I'm seduced by the waves
a perfect break on a bar, I'm naked and brave.

Cold pristine water, glistening white sand I'm
drawn to liquid sapphire and depart the land
wading in to this magical lure
I boldly plunge into the ancient milieu.

Such a magical way to enter this medium
to escape life's troubles and its tedium
engulfed immediately by multiple sensations
I begin to stroke with breathless exhilaration.

Clearness, sharpness it hits you as one
adrenaline surges and its always fun
to be dumped and rolled in salty white foam
on a beautiful beach so far from home.

I confidently glide over restless crests
scanning the calm bottom for nasty pests
crabs and whiting have a good stare
at an ungainly nude in their lair.

A skinny dip in the Tasman is somehow surreal
unencumbered, unburdened it's a primitive appeal
a cleansing freedom and spiritual meditation
my skin and mind tingle with excitation.

I ponder the positives and the anticipation
of being a sea mammal, a worthy consideration of
a life hereafter on Tasmania's coast and a
return to the ocean through reincarnation.

Possibles v Probables

A Great Britain Rugby League Team toured Australia and New Zealand in 1966. It played 30 games in the three month trip. One game was played in Cooma against a combined Monaro Division team on Sunday 31st July at Rotary Oval in front of a crowd of 6,000 spectators. It was a freezing, windy day that reminded me of a line in the poem 'The Coachman' by EJ Brady about the Monaro.

'Cold as charity, cold as hell; bleak bare barren Nimmitabel; Nimmitabel on the Monaro.'

As a curtain-raiser to the International clash a team of Under 18s 'Possibles' from Group 16 (Far South Coast and Bega Valley) played the 'Probables' from Group 19 (Snowy Mountains and Monaro region). A combined team of the best of the Under 18 players was to be announced at half-time of the International match. This was my big chance for fame in the tough world of country rugby league.

I had just begun playing league, until then preferring basketball as a winter sport as I tried to avoid injury that may have hindered my swimming career. I began with the Under 18 Bega Roosters and surprisingly was selected after 4 games in the Possibles as a prop forward in the Group 16 team.

We all strived for selection. I held a glimmer of hope that a scout from North Sydney RLFC would be watching, contract in hand, to woo me to play with Billy Wilson and Lloyd Weier in the Red and Black front row. But alas, there was to be no Bears academy for me.

We ran out onto a dry tussocked ground trying hard to display toughness, durability and skill. But when the opposition team lined up opposite for the perfunctory handshake, all confidence and hope drained from me. These players were not boys, they were men, seemingly taller, wider and thicker than any of us. We were a team of lily-white surfer boys with soft skin and measley muscles.

The Monaro team kicked off, a towering place kick that our fullback, a skinny kid from Eden with a Russell Fairfax hairstyle dropped in front of the posts. A scrum was set. I looked up to assess my opposite number. He was a farm boy from Bibbenluke, who had rolled the sleeves of his jersey up to reveal his massive, hairy forearms. We packed the scrum and he grabbed my jersey with callused, vice-like hands. I tried to hold by digging in my studs, but the Brute from Bibbenluke pushed me backward and screwed the scrum. Another scrum was set. This time, in an act of provocation, aggression and power he rubbed his man-stubble up my cheek and across my temple. I was outraged and protested to the referee. My facial hair was bum fluff and his whiskers were like steel spikes. I thought my skin had been scraped off with coarse sandpaper. I swung a punch at him in frustration. After I protested to the ref he told me to toughen up, that I was a front-rower after all.

He cautioned me, awarded a penalty and their fullback from the Snowy River Bears club at Jindabyne kicked the goal. It was not a good start. It only got worse. Back in those days of unlimited tackles, before the 'modern era' any team that could hold the ball, maintained possession. At times, it meant that one team may be forced to tackle for 15 or 20 minutes. And so it was that the 'possibles from the coast' became the would-be tacklers of the 'probables from the mountains,' only to have the bigger, stronger, faster Monaro boys run through us.

At half time, the Monaro probables had an unassailable lead. Our coach, a former Balmain Tiger, suggested that instead of taking them on 'up the middle,' we should swing the ball wide and give the backs a run. That suited me because I was happier being a ball-playing front rower rather then a tackling turnstile. Every time I got the ball I passed it, except once when I saw an opening, threw a dummy and lumbered through a gap the size of the Sydney Heads. But I was quickly cut down by the Bombala lock forward in a scything tackle. I crashed to the ground and the ball rolled loose. It was picked up by their menacing, rangy second rower from Dalgety, who scored. I feigned injury and was replaced, doleful of my woeful attempt at selection in representative footy.

Our 'strapper,' a self-taught masseur from Bemboka consoled me. He suggested that many of the opposition players were older than eighteen, that Group 19 had cheated in picking their 'probables' team. They were like men who worked on farms, used to throwing bales of hay, fleeces or sacks of feed like the Brute from Bibbenluke. By contrast, my work to date had been practising tumble-turns in the Bega Pool. How could I possibly compete against a farm labourer?

After showering in cold water in the windy corrugated iron changing rooms, I sat on a bench devouring two hot pies with sauce and can of passiona (we did not have a dietitian to advise us of post match nutrition). I watched the Poms go through their paces against the grown up men of the Monaro Division. The Lions fielded their second team and won 33-12.

The Combined Under 18 team was announced over loudspeakers as part of the half-time entertainment which consisted of the 8 piece Cooma Town Band playing 40s and 50s hits. I was not among the squad, but the Brute for Bibbenluke was named captain. Worthy, I'm sure!

Sasha's Coffee Sanctum

Ristretto

The aroma of freshly brewed coffee on this cool Moscow morning was appealing. Like a beagle, I followed my nose down Taverskaya Street towards Red Square. The cafe was squeezed between imposing grey government office blocks. I had not come across an espresso bar like this in Russia before, although Starbucks outlets seemed to be proliferating like cancer. But I avoided these and similar franchise chains because of their sickening syrups, plastic spoons and paper cups.

The variety of small coffee pots, percolators and syphon filters sitting on glass shelves was intriguing. There were no labels or prices, but definitely a 'look at me' Italianesque attitude. From inside I heard the screech of milk being frothed and saw a shining espresso machine belching steam. I then knew that this coffee would be worth tasting.

Two earnest young men wearing white shirts and tight black trousers busied themselves. Their haircuts were pure George Harrison chic and they were both were clean shaven, unlike many Russian men whose designer stubble or beards masked their faces and expressions. Slim, strong and fit in an aesthetic manner, they exuded vitality and health. Their appearance gave me the impression they were serious about their looks and lifestyle.

Their cafe mode rocked short leather aprons with braces edged with emerald. It was a masculine difference to the usual loop around the neck and emphasised the muscle definition of their broad shoulders reminding me of gymnasts' builds.

'I'd like a double ristretto please,' ready to point to the menu if needed.

The striking young barista looked me in the eye, tilted his head like a magpie listening for grubs, paused and then nodded.

'Yes, of course, sir. Please take a seat and I will bring it out to you,' he responded in perfect English.

Despite the morning rush of workers picking up a takeaway, the crockery and cutlery gleamed, tabletops glistened and the spotless floor veritably squeaked. The cafe's vibe was anything but hipster grunge and the prices indicated their targeted up-market clients.

In no time at all he returned with a steaming cup of aromatic, chocolate-coloured crema and slid effortlessly into the opposite chair. Before I had a chance to taste, he was blurting out.

'We want to go to the Mardi Gras in Sydney. Do you know of it? Can you help me come?' His face was intense and expectant.

I was taken aback by his rapid nailing of my accent to boldly slip in such a question as a conversation starter. We chatted about the Gay and Lesbian Mardi Gras but I wasn't able to tell him very much.

'Sasha, help please!' The voice of the other young man was high, maybe in the contralto range and the tone was semi-urgent. Sasha raised his palm to ask me to say put. I nodded.

He filled some orders then returned with a gift.

'I'm sorry. I was quite rude earlier. My name is Sasha. Welcome to my Sanctum. I am very pleased to have our first Australian customer. Thank you for coming in. Please have this on our behalf.'

I nodded and smiled my appreciation at the Danish before

me. Between orders for macchiatos, lattes and cappuccinos he kept returning, eager to share his life story and ambitions.

Long Black

In partnership with his lover, Anatoly, they'd established the cafe six months earlier after months of planning and negotiations. Neither of the boy's families knew they were gay. They'd been guarded about the relationship, fearing adverse consequences should it be revealed. In Russia, homosexual conduct was illegal and strictly amoral according to the powerful Russian Orthodox Church.

'Though gay marriage has been legalised in many countries, even in Australia now, this is not the case here in conservative, Orthodox Russia.'

I had taken a passing interest in Putin's growing conservatism and the increasing number of 'crackdowns' on dissenters of the regime's policies that inhibited freedom and human rights. I knew about the international opprobrium towards Putin and his security forces when the all female band, Pussy Riot, challenged the system through pop music and public performances.

'Lesbians and gays are still forced to meet clandestinely, especially in regional and rural areas for fear of bashings and even arrest. In Moscow and St Petersburg there is some tolerance. We have a few gay clubs, but we have to be very careful.'

Gay and lesbian couples could be seen swooning, holding hands and embracing on the warm spring evenings. Others in the park were not staring or protesting and the lovers were unguarded about their behaviour. It seemed the same in any other European city.

Sasha was an outgoing, confident young man who welcomed

customers from behind his frothing machine. Anatoli was an introvert, more beautiful and mysteriously aloof. He fussed over the tables, collected empties and washed cups, saucers and cutlery assiduously.

'We met at ballet school in St Petersburg at age twelve. My family is rich and well connected here in Moscow. They paid my fees to attend. Anatoly is from a poor and religious family in rural Tvir Provence. He won a scholarship because of his natural talent. He is so beautiful when he dances.'

Despite the privileged ballet training, neither rose to great heights. They were unable to sustain themselves financially from short contracts with regional ballet companies or from occasional seasons in France or Italy.

Sasha then convinced his father to fund the coffee business despite the expensive start-up costs. The business plan included the purchase of the latest Italian espresso machine with barista training in Rome for three weeks. His father also reluctantly agreed to meet the cost of rent for a shop in the heart of the financial and tourist precinct for twelve months while the boys established their reputation as a high-end coffee destination.

I watched the two young men squeeze around each other to serve customers. It was a small space behind the counter and their legs, hips and arms constantly touched. They were comfortable being close, sometimes brushing each other's clothes or adjusting each other's wide leather apron straps.

Sasha's Coffee Sanctum became my Moscow morning sanctuary. It was easy to chat freely with the 'boys' as I referred to them in my head. They had pluck and I had no qualms about inviting them to Sydney. Sasha gratefully received my business card.

Cappuccino

Every Friday evening in their chic apartment, Sasha reclined in his black leather chaise lounge while Anatoli treated him to a foot and leg massage. It had become a treasured ritual along with a glass or two of their favourite Georgian shiraz. Sasha loved being massaged and Anatoli revelled in the tactile. As well as the sensuous, the boys discussed customers, trading figures and issues that Anatoli described as 'efficiency matters.'

'Sash, we are not doing as well as our business plan forecast,' Anatoli announced. 'Our monthly income is barely covering costs and we are not yet drawing our proper wages! We really need to be selling much more coffee. Sasha, are you listening to me?'

He sounded cross and serious and paused massaging so that Sasha might concentrate on these substantive business matters. He often thought that Sasha was too hedonistic to be a good businessman.

There was an extended silence between them and the background classical music became intrusive. Anatoli resumed the rubbing while waiting for Sasha's response.

'Why can't we take orders from the offices close by and offer a delivery service? Most of our customers work in these buildings and we can ask them to tell their colleagues about having coffee at their desks. I can get Vlad to design a leaflet for distribution and maybe we could even have an App to receive orders and payment. Remember in Rome, in that little cafe down in the Eur? They even had a guy deliver them on a Vespa with a special rack to transport the cups. It was so cool.'

'Please don't rush ahead with all these ideas, Sasha. We have to take it step-by-step. The App sounds good, but the costs could be massive,' Anatoli countered.

'Just leave it to me for a few days and I'll do some research. There's a Start-Up near the Metropole Hotel that does Web and App development. Let me talk to them.'

Latte

The following Friday as they started their second glass of wine, Sasha proposed a new marketing strategy.

'We've never launched the Sanctum, have we Toli? We've never gone after publicity or splashed our name about. We were happy to let it grow organically – and it has! But as you say, the business is struggling and I think, like you, it needs a boost.'

Anatoli squeezed the calf more firmly, a message to Sasha that he was listening.

'I've seen my friends at the communications company. They would be very happy to design an App for Sasha's Coffee Sanctum, using our logo and colours and manage the payment with our bank.'

'But how much would that cost, Sash?' Anatoli fretted about debt and about Sasha's father who he felt was over-bearing when he discussed business progress with the boys.

'They'll do it on a commission basis. No upfront cost, but they would take a percentage of the sales via the App.'

'So a successful App strategy benefits us both. A win-win as the Americans say?' Anatoli was warming to the idea. 'What percentage will they take Sasha?'

'That is to be negotiated as the project develops. Don't worry Toli, they are good, young people like us and they want to see us succeed.'

'Samara, who is their marketing guru suggested launching the App one evening and inviting our customers, suppliers and friends. And I am proposing that we have an exhibition of your drawings at the same time to bring in some extra income. What do you think Toli?'

'Please don't bring my artwork up again Sasha. We are in the coffee business, not sketches and drawings. Besides, a public showing of my fantasies is not what I want.'

Anatoli kneaded the foot faster and and more vigorously as he thought about this idea. It frightened him and he continued to protect his drawings.

'But Sasha, they are not for the public. My sketchings are private and I would be embarrassed if our friends and customers saw them. In any case, we could be charged under Putin's new law of displaying homosexual propaganda.'

'Toli, your drawings are world-class erotica and I am sure that many of our friends would pay a lot to hang them on their walls. Why not use your talents to boost the business?'

Quiet and introverted, Anatoli did not respond immediately. He detested arguing with the outgoing and confident Sasha. He considered his sketches to be intimate and he did not want others to gawk at the charcoal and crayon works.

Anatoli's hands moved up Sasha's smooth waxed leg to his generous calf. He adored feeling the warmth, suppleness and weight of Sasha's gastrocnemius. He nursed them with both hands, stroking the almond oil from the achilles up to the knee.

The days lengthened as spring sunshine continued to thaw winter blues. So too did the plan for a launch of their initiative and art exhibition. Leaflets were handed to customers and distributed to nearby office blocks and shops.

Corporate Coffee and Art
INVITATION
Thursday 26 April 2019
5:00 - 8:00pm
Sasha's Coffee Sanctum
118 Taverskaya Avenue
An evening of coffee, wine & surprise
Expect the Unexpected
RSVP by text to Samara 0678 275689

'I don't think our shop is big enough,' Anatoli said to Sasha. 'Already fifty people have said they'll be coming. What are we going to do?' His voice was loaded with angst.

'They won't all come at the same time Toli. We'll manage, and I've asked Max and Vlad to help us. It's going to be fun and our business will boom. Just wait and see.

'Samara has a brochure about how to use the App and will project it onto the wall so people can see what they have to do. The orders will come in on our iPad and process the money directly into the bank account. How good is that?'

Sasha was excited by the coming event, the attention it would bring to the business and hopefully more sales.

Anatoli had reluctantly agreed to exhibit his drawings after he had shown them to Samara who was full of praise and reminded him of how his Babushka used to extol his talents. As a child in the country he had sketched flowers, birds and farm animals and on her visits, his grandmother praised his drawings and talent. She was always encouraging and brought him gifts of sketchpads, pencils and crayons.

Starting ballet at age seven, he sketched classmates. With maturity his art became more sensual and in teenage years he drew images of the human form that aroused him sexually.

But he never showed these sketch books to anyone, holding them locked in a trunk under his bed. They were always secret until he met Sasha, and now Samara. So to display them publicly was a monumental step, strange and threatening.

'Samara is very nice, isn't she Sash? She's helped me so much in getting my drawings organised and even arranged framing. I couldn't do that myself. She suggested the ones to exhibit and picked different sizes, different bodies and not too much of the 'sleaze' as you call it.'

'I really hope you've included the triptych, Toli. There should be a premium price on that.'

'Samara will conduct a silent auction. People can bid by placing their names on a sheet. That way we can get a good idea of their market value.'

'What about the triptych Toli, is it in?'

'I'm worried about the people coming. They don't know us and it could cause a lot of problems.' Anatoli's anxiety was rising because he would be revealing his innermost secrets.

'Almost everyone who's responded are young, professional and well-educated, Toli. They accept gays and I think it's OK for us to show our colours. It can be our 'coming out' show. As if they didn't know already.'

Two days were spent preparing the long narrow space. Fifteen selected drawings were hung. Round tables with white and perfectly pressed table clothes were placed down the centre of the room each adorned with a vase of freshly cut flowers. The brochures for the App were spread for easy pickup.

Soy Latte with Cinnamon

Their customers comprised young professional Muscovites. Each morning, sipping my ristretto, I was impressed by the style of men, and especially the women, who came in for their morning fix. The females were expensively dressed, slim and elegant in posture. Pants suits or pencil skirts were figure-hugging, hair styles immaculately neat and jewellery was discreet and expensive. Heels oozed class and dare I say it, sex.

Often they carried a shoulder bag with a laptop and an Italian designer handbag with matching shoes. They were business-like, aloof and very attractive, to me at least. Sometimes one or two would glance my way with indifference, perhaps, wondering who this stranger was.

One morning a diminutive young women bounced in, beaming at Sasha.

'Good morning Sash! Hi Toli! We've made great progress on your App and have a working version that we plan to test in the next few days. I hope we can show you on Friday.' Her voice was full of enthusiasm and confidence.

She glanced over, then looked at Sasha. 'Is this your friend from Australia?'

'Yes, it is, please come and meet him.'

'Phillip, this is our designer, Samara. I've told her about you and how you've been helping Toli and me with business development.'

I stood to engage this striking young woman who confidently shook my hand and looked straight into my eyes.

'I'm very pleased to meet you, Philippe. Welcome to Moscow! It's so nice to see that you've found the best coffee in the city.' Her eyes were light blue and her skin incandescent and unblemished. She was beautiful and it occurred to me she could have been a famous ballerina or even a super model if she were taller.

'Lovely to meet you, Samara. I've heard a lot about you.' I responded in what sounded to me like my broad, boring, flat accent.

'Will you be coming to the opening next week?'

'Well, I've been invited but I'm not sure it's my scene. I'm more than happy with my morning coffee and a chat with the boys.'

'Oh, you must come, even if it is just to see Toli's drawings, they are very special.' Samara said in an inviting manner. 'I'd love to see you there.'

Then she was gone. I returned to my coffee to contemplate the encounter with Samara. She was indeed the perfect, persuasive PR person.

Double Shot Espresso

Their gay friends, Vlad and Max arrived early in dinner suits to serve guests French champagne, vodka, Georgian wine or Peroni as they arrived.

When I arrived for the Friday evening launch, the Sanctum was bustling with gossiping guests. Champagne flutes dinged as greetings were exchanged. Apart from Sasha and Anatoli I knew no one, but I was soon engaged by Samara.

'Have you seen Anatoli's sketches yet?' she asked with raised eyebrows. I gently shook my head.

'Are you interested in Arte d'Erotique, Philippe?'

'Let's go take a look,' she purred, not waiting for my answer, and placed her arm in mine, as if we were old friends. We glided past the drinks table, scooped up a flute each then stopped at the first drawing. It was a hyper-masculine figure with tight black shorts, braces and small leather cap. Anatoli's depiction of musculature seemed to be perfect.

'Anatoli explained to me how the famous gay artist, Tom of Finland, had influenced his work. He found the book about Tom in a secondhand bookshop and was immediately taken by his 'hyper-masculinised' drawings,' Samara explained with raised eyebrows.

I nodded, hardly believing that I was being given a guided tour of homoerotic art by a breathtakingly attractive young woman who held my arm whilst nestling in closer to my side. The waft of her perfume was subtle and disconcertingly alluring.

The drawing of a square-jawed man with rippling abs showed pectorals with strikingly erect nipples. A small black captain's hat on his head emphasised broad facial features. Tight leather hot pants strained to contain the bulge between thick thighs.

Other drawings showed one or two male figures in provocative poses. Most sketches did not show the genitalia but the art did not leave much to the imagination.

We sauntered along before pausing in front of a charcoal sketch of a stylised, naked, long-legged woman in high, thin stilettos admiring herself in a full-length mirror. Her frontal reflection was an exaggerated image of herself. It was an interesting technique and the female body was bare for all to see.

'How much is this one do you think?' I asked my escort.

'I thought you may be interested in this one,' she whispered close to my ear. Her cheeky smile revealed a flirtatious nature. 'Let's look later at the bidding sheet and you can make a play for her, perhaps?'

I tried to decipher her ambiguous answer when she squeezed my arm. We glanced at the range of Anatoli's erotica depicting dancers, bodies and private parts. Samara did not try and talk above all the gasping and guffawing, but she stayed close enough for me to feel the heat of her body.

On the back wall a cluster of admirers was ogling at three frames placed together.

'This is the piece d'resistance Philippe – the triptych,' declared Samara, shouldering her way in for a clearer view, pulling me along with her.

'OH MY GOD,' a young woman clad in a short leather skirt and fishnets cried out, drawing attention to herself. She immediately placed her hand over her mouth and turned to find her friend in the crowded room.

'Leyla, quickly, come and look at this!' and she dragged her scantily dressed friend by the hand towards the three nested artworks. 'This is so HOT!'

The three drawings of the triptych were startling and confronting.

'God, I love it. I like the look of his equipment.' Leila's surreptitious smile showed how much she was enjoying the titillating artworks.

Unbeknown, the two young women had now become the 'objets d'art' themselves. Nearby guests sniggered and moved back to allow a space for the two girls who were wholly immersed in their admiration of the enticing bodies on display.

'Wait till you see the centre piece!'

Samara's arm tightened around mine, anticipating the unknown. She was smiling and enjoying the ad-hoc entertainment.

'Have you seen it?' I asked.

'Oh yes, on many occasions actually. I had to convince Anatoli that he should show it. The concession I reached with him was the silk cloth to hide the masculinity. But now, as you can see, hiding the phallus is actually contributing to the mystique and allure.'

Nadia, with a flourish, tore the velcro, the modesty drape fell away. Someone gasped, others giggled, while a male voice hooted.

The image was powerful. The upper body and face were turned away, but Anatoli had been able to portray the beautiful strong curves of the deltoids and biceps. The lower portion was frontal and its centre piece was striking, glistening and tumescent. The chatter in the room grew louder and spontaneously there was yelping and applause.

'Fully locked and loaded eh brother?' remarked a wag to his partner.

Macchiato

At the end of the evening Sasha and Anatoli sat with Max, Vlad, Samara and myself with flutes of chilled, French champagne. They all smiled as they raised their glasses in congratulations. We all enjoyed the fresh, tingling bubbles.

As I was preparing to leave, the front door was flung open. Six men and two women walked into the cafe and surrounded us. They all looked similar – thick-set, short hair, besuited with open necked dark shirts and conspicuous earpieces. One stepped forward and showed his police badge.

The officers then went to work, photographing the artworks before removing them; gathering the bid sheets with guest names and phone numbers; frisking us; asking for identification and photographing each of us.

Humiliated, we were frog marched onto the footpath and pushed into the back of a police bus. No one spoke, as we were all so stunned. We'd gone from the high of a successful, convivial, joyful launch to the depths of cold, distant, Russian detention.

After being held in a cell overnight, I was driven to Domodedovo Airport and escorted onto an Aeroflot jet for Istanbul, thence Turkish Airlines to Sydney. At departure I was handed my passport, a ticket and informed tersely by the smart, uniformed, female border control officer that I was not welcome in Russia again and that my visa had been cancelled.

Outraged but helpless, I had to accept this stark act of Russian authoritarianism in action. It was a matter of me being in the wrong place at the wrong time. But I was terribly worried about my new Russian friends. What would be their fate?

Affogato

Eighteen months later, all was revealed when I opened an email with a mail.ru stem. It was from Sasha. Could I pick him up from Kingsford Smith on Sunday night and accommodate him until he found his feet? His sign off message was: 'I have so much to tell you!'

Waiting in the arrivals hall, I was unsure of what to expect as I watched bedraggled passengers from international flights push their luggage trolleys into the crowd. Lost in thought, I was startled by Sasha who suddenly appeared. We embraced without speaking. He held me close for what seemed like minutes.

'You remember Anatoli?' Sasha turned and reached for his partner's hand, urging him forward. I hardly recognised the whippet-thin, bald, prematurely aged Toli. I hugged him, but he seemed lifeless. At home, as we sipped hot chocolate and nibbled Anzac biscuits, their story unfolded.

Sasha had spent four days in detention until he was released after his father intervened at a political level with substantial cash collateral. He resumed life in St Petersburg working between coffee houses and restaurants while he pursued his application for a visa to come to Australia, a country far enough away from the country of his birth that he now despised.

Anatoli was sent to a labour camp in Siberia, his crime being, 'Sedition through the creation and perpetuation of blasphemous homosexual material.' In a prison with hardened criminals, long monotonous work routines and harsh conditions, Anatoli almost withered away. When other inmates discovered he was gay, he was brutalised. After twelve months of internment, he was released into Sasha's care.

It seemed to me that Toli needed food, rest and much love and affection. With help from my contacts in the health system, Anatoli's rehabilitation began. Over time he regained some strength and with Sasha's care they began to meet some friends in Sydney's gay community.

The two young men began to rent an apartment in North Bondi. Anatoli, after gaining social confidence and improved language skills, is working casually in local restaurants, assisted by the Eastern Suburbs Russian community. Sasha has begun teaching dance at the 'School of Arts Ballet School.' But not only ballet – Latin and pump aerobics as well! His popular classes are packed with adoring young mums and fawning gay men.

They were part of the 'Bondi Lifesavers' float at the recent LGBTQI festival and danced the night away at the Hordern Pavilion. They are saving to buy a coffee shop in Coogee and will be naming it 'Sasha's Coffee Sanctum.'

Flat White

On their night of arrival, Sasha handed me a lemon-coloured envelope. The calligraphic 'Philippe' on the front was sufficient for me to know who the sender was. Then I smelt the perfume. The memory of Samara's warm body next to mine on the night of the Sanctum opening engaged my senses once more through this distinctive aroma.

'Mon Bon Ami Philippe,

I trust this letter finds you healthy and happy. I'm sorry that I cannot say the same for myself. After I saw you on that fateful night, I was detained for six weeks by the Police. They charged me with being an accessory to the crime of Sedition. I was released after representations to the court by the lawyers engaged to defend me.

I've been working hard for the last 12 months trying to pay the company back and to build the business, but my heart has been broken from the shock of the police bust we all experienced. Sasha has been a great support, visiting me on his trips back to moscow from St Petersburg and encouraging me to think about moving on from Russia.

We seemed to be making good progress with our freedoms here. There was more tolerance shown towards young people and their views. We were connected to the world via the internet and were able to shop internationally. You have no idea what it was like for girls like me to be able to wear smart western fashion – a liberation.

Putin is tightening the reins slowly like it was during Stalin's repulsive soviet system – oppression.

Philippe, you seemed such a nice, kind, handsome man. I really enjoyed your company and I know the boys appreciated your friendship. When Sasha told me he had won the visa to

Australia, I wanted to write to you to re-establish our connection. I, too, want to come to Australia. It is such a wonderful country. Can you help me please?

Unfortunately, I do not have the qualifications, skills or money to get enough points for a work visa. Nor do I have connections like Sasha. So I want to ask if you could offer to marry me in order to enter your country? I know this is a bold question, but I am desperately lonely, scared and full of despair.

Enclosed is a recent photo. You'll see that I look a little bit thinner but I have not lost my figure. I want you to have it to remember me. I have just been able to establish an internet account and I'll look everyday for your response to my letter. Then we can exchange some good messages and photos.

It will be fun to have an Aussie friend and I look forward to sharing an iced coffee with you on Bondi beach.

Avec amour bronzed Aussie

Samara
Xoxoxo

El Niño

Peruvian fishermen call him el Niño by name
the problem boy child who they say is to blame
for their dwindling catch of seafood and fishes
and the death of anchovies against their wishes.

He brings too much warm water this problematic colt
disrupting the ecology of the cold Humboldt
trade winds and currents alter their positions
the globe's climate produces unappealing conditions.

Our warming Pacific creates a weird meteorology
it's measured incessantly with advanced technology
the cyclones and typhoons are much more frequent
their power and impact has more deadly intent.

Greenhouse gases cause the globe to heat
and when absorbed by the ocean it's hard to defeat
a rise in sea levels, strange atmospheric events
Can we implement change and hopefully prevent?

Many people implore us and some try to inspire
while our government and miners seem to conspire
against the reduction of fossil fuel burning
when for renewables is what we're all yearning.

For while anchovies are not our favourite meal
they're our contemporary canaries and that should appeal
to us all to heed this message of warning
and slow up this trend of global warming.

The Venezuelan Cartel

We were late for the 4pm departure, having underestimated the time, and the cost, of a taxi ride from Manhattan to Pier 9A. The First Mate met us at the bottom of the gangway, checked our passports and welcomed us aboard. Dropping our backpacks in Cabin 3 Portside, we joined our fellow passengers on the viewing deck, just below the blue and white striped funnel of the Royal Netherlands Freighter Company's *MS Socrates*.

It was a mixed bunch – all seven of them. A middle-aged couple from Illinois, Geoffrey, a pipe smoking, small town lawyer and his demure wife Helen assailed us with questions. Both oozed conservatism, from their beige pants and cardigans to their conversation. They were ruing the defeat of Gerald Ford, replaced instead by the 'peanut growing' Democrat from Georgia, Jimmy Carter. We were cross examined with forensic like enquiries from Geoffrey about our heritage, intent and motivations. Fortunately, the one-sided conversation ended when we were interrupted by Dorothy,

'Call me Dot.'

She'd heard our Australian accent and excitedly interjected. Dot was recovering from the recent death of her husband and was travelling alone. From Florida, she was as 'sweet as apple pie' and when she learnt we were both Physical Education teachers, she told us how she loved Nadia Comaneci, who four weeks earlier, had won 5 gold medals at the 1976 Montreal Olympics. We came to love Dot over the five weeks we spent on the Socrates, as she loved us.

The ship still hadn't departed, although it didn't stop Geoffrey from grumbling about the late sailing time. He went off seeking an explanation for the delay and returned to inform all that we were still waiting for one passenger, a Venezuelan businessman. Forty minutes later we heard a car door slam below. Peeking over the railing we watched a stout man with yellow shirt, jacket, black rimmed glasses and thinning hair walk toward the gangway.

At the top of the gangway he was greeted by the Captain as if old friends. The tardy businessman presented the Captain with a bottle of Black Label Johnny Walker from his overnight bag. He also carried a burnished brown briefcase with gold latches and hinges. Soon after, the *Socrates'* horn blasted just above our heads, the hawsers were slipped from their bollards and we glided into the channel of New York Harbour.

The 7,000 ton, 130m *Socrates* sailed past the Statue of Liberty, through the Narrows of New York Bay and into the sunset, before we adjourned to the dining room for a three-course meal in the company of our fellow passengers. Who knows what they thought of two 26 year olds with our shorts, leather sandals and backpacks?

Guests at Captain Van Djik's table were a father and his eccentric son from California. The overconfident young man persisted in boring the Captain about a new computer company called Apple. The big Dutchman with a ruddy face took larger mouthfuls of his whisky every time the Ph.D. (Physics UCLA) candidate spoke.

At another table flopped a sozzled, loud, over-bangled New Yorker with her ancient 'Personal Physician,' to whom she was completely addicted. We learnt that two or three Bloody Marys before lunch was standard practice for Susana and, after a bottle of wine over lunch, she'd pass out for most of the afternoon before resuming with Martinis at 4.00pm. We were informed that Robert, 84 years, was a former senior John Hopkins physician who prescribed alcohol at will to his rich patient. Their dependence on each other was palpable.

The Venezuelan businessman dined alone which made him more conspicuous. Noting his liberal use of pimento and nutmeg on the chicken breast, green beans, pumpkin and mashed potato, he devoured the meal and departed. He did not take advantage of the ships' duty free liquor, unlike me. Heineken beer was 25c a bottle, the tab payable at the end of the cruise.

Adjusting to the rock and roll of the ship and the thrum of its engines took some time as we lay on our bunkbeds awaiting sleep. It would not be the first time we wondered what we were doing. Marie's serendipitous glance at a *New York Times* advertisement four days previously for 'Freighter Travel' for ten passengers was too good to be true. We had jumped at the opportunity for passage, accommodation and food for five weeks for $US500 each. Now, in this small cabin, in the middle of the ocean, I wondered if we should have chosen the Greyhound bus and headed for New Orleans instead.

Early next morning I awoke with the sun streaming directly onto my face through the porthole. I slipped out of my bunk, dressed, and navigated my way to the bow. To my surprise the businessman was already there enjoying the glorious Caribbean Sea along with percolated coffee and a croissant. He greeted me warmly, proffering his hand and offered his name, 'Eduardo Jimenez.'

His conversational English surprised me and with my crude Spanish, we managed to chat. Fascinated that we were Australian he wanted to know about our government, politics and agriculture. It was one of many discussions with him where I found myself ignorant of how my country operated. When Marie joined us, we chatted like friends, sharing stories of our families, study and work.

The turbulent politics of the Caribbean and South American countries were often topics he raised. He believed the future of Cuba was unclear because the 'rebel communist, Fidel Castro' had gained control. When he learnt that we intended to travel to Argentina he spoke to us about Isabel Peron being deposed and the right-wing military government now running the country. Similarly in Chile, General Pinochet had taken over and the country was now in dictatorship.

Our youthful ignorance was bliss at the time, but we soon learnt that soldiers holding guns on guard at banks, government offices and bus terminals were commonplace in many countries. 'Peacekeepers,' we were informed by leaflets thrust into our passports at border crossings. It didn't worry us, and apart from the unfolding mystery of Señor Jimenez, our trip was trouble free of the law, but not of misadventure.

After two days we berthed at our first port of call, Santo Domingo, the capital of the Dominican Republic which occupies two-thirds of the island it shares with Haiti. Two Cadillacs for the President were unloaded from the upper deck, along with assorted crates, boxes and nets of miscellaneous items from below.

Señor Jimenez invited us to lunch in the city, along with our new friend Dot. A taxi met us on the dock and we ate spicy sizzling steak and chipped sweet potatoes at an open air restaurant. During the meal he told us that he chose freighter travel for his import/export business trips to the US for health reasons. Flying didn't agree with him.

I took out a traveller's cheque to contribute to the cost of the meal, but he pushed my hand away. Instead, he left a crisp $US50.00 note on the table without asking for the bill and we walked away completely satiated, inwardly smug because of the free feast and impressed with our new benefactor.

Further ports of call included Porto Cabello in Venezuela, Port of Spain in Trinidad, Georgetown in Guyana, Paramaribo in Surinam and Cuidad Bolivar, a port on the Orinoco River in Venezuela, 400km upstream. At all these locations we could leave the ship for a day's sight seeing in the countryside or shopping at markets with the local people. In Port of Spain street markets we ate, for the first time in our lives, fresh feijoas, guavas and sipped from coconuts.

Marie noticed intriguing designs of leather sandals at a corner stall. She asked the tall, handsome Rastafarian artisan if she might try a pair. While she sat on his wooden crate, he held her shapely calf in his big soft left hand and skilfully glided the *huarache* onto her foot, attended to the straps and repeated his silent seductive-like actions with her other foot. I begrudgingly signed a travellers cheque for the over-priced, impractical footwear.

Señor Jimenez was due to disembark the ship at Porto Cabello, one of Venezuela's main ports. Before leaving he encouraged us to visit him and meet his family in the nearby city of Barquisimeto the following weekend. The Captain had informed us that there would be a ten-day wait at anchor in the bay before docking due to congestion at the port and that we were free to explore.

On Friday morning the small tender dropped us ashore. When we arrived at his home after a train journey we were welcomed warmly by his wife and three teenage children. The weekend sight seeing and restaurant tour, all at the Señor's expense, were paid for with fresh US bank notes. I began to wonder why the businessman was not using Bolivars in his home town.

On Saturday he received two men at his home. As I walked

along the hallway toward the bathroom, I happened to glance into his office. The men were conversing in Español and the burnished, brown brief case with golden locks and hinges was open on his desk. My eyes were drawn to the contents and stalled me. I stared in wonder. They were not files or folders as I'd expected in a business portfolio, but bundles of stacked American $50 dollar notes. He held two bundles in his hand and was offering them to the men. On the floor was a hessian sack.

The Señor walked toward me, stood very close and glared into my eyes. Gone was the warm open face, replaced with a cold, threatening glower. Without looking away he tapped his nose with the forefinger of his right hand. This simple, powerful gesture conveyed to me that I was now complicit in his business activities, and that I should remain silent or there could be serious consequences.

We felt like prisoners, inadvertently ensnared in international cocaine trafficking. In the days before mobile telephones or WiFi no one in the world knew where we were. We were untraceable and if Señor Jimenez or his associates wished us to disappear, then we could be easily dispatched by a member of his cartel and our bodies dumped in the Orinoco River to be torn apart by piranhas.

Señor Jimenez was well connected. His brother was the Minister for Agriculture and it was arranged that we would return to the port with the Minister in his government car, chauffeur driven before the Parliament resumed on Monday. We had a running commentary of the beef industry, the black beans growing in the adjacent paddocks and the laziness of workers in Venezuela.

On Sunday afternoon the sea had changed its mood. Very large swells were crossing the bay and they looked ominous as sunset approached, casting long shadows from the peaking waves. The anchored ships, including the *Socrates*, appeared a long way from shore, rising and falling in the swell.

Surprisingly the gangplank had been hoisted to the deck, deemed too dangerous to use. Instead, seamen threw a rope ladder over the side. We understood that we would have to climb the sheer five meter side of the ship. Tying our backpacks to ropes that were then pulled to safety above, we listened to instructions in Spanish from the Master of the tender.

Our own risk analysis informed us of the danger of the quick ascent required. A gymnastic 'spring' from the back of the tender onto the ladder and ascend quickly before the small boat rose with a swell and crushed our legs. We looked up and saw the faces of crewmen waiting to assist us at the top of the ladder. Our physical education skills had never been more important.

Marie was to go first, but she demurred, preferring to wait for a perfect moment for take off, as was her prerogative. My impetuousness prevailed and I rushed past her, grabbed the ladder and began the ascent. But as I'd taken off at the bottom of a swell, the rise of the next swell brought the tender up and into the side of the ship much faster than I was climbing. My left foot was crushed between the stern of the tender and the steel of the ship's side, as well as cracking and splintering three or four wooden rungs.

I held on tightly and glanced down to see four toes of my left foot angled at forty-five degrees, twisted, gnarled and blood splattered. My tourist sandals had offered no protection. Now I was in no-man's land. The small boat had pulled away, the skipper fearing another impact and injury. I had four metres to climb with two hands and one good foot and leg. I did not want to drop into the ocean. Up I scampered, until I felt strong hands grab both my arms and pull me up and over onto the deck. I then fainted, disappearing from Marie's sight.

Early that evening I was visited in my cabin by the elderly Physician. He diagnosed broken toes, prescribed aspirin and to told me to keep my foot raised. The next morning the sea had abated and after an uncomfortable night, we were lowered by crane in a cargo net to the back of the tender. An 'ambulance' met us and we were placed in the back of a dusty international panel van for the short trip to a 'health clinic.'

The local GP in Puerto Cabello assessed the x-rays revealing the four crooked toes were twisted and cracked. He then proceeded to wrap the foot and lower leg in bandages of Plaster of Paris. I asked and gestured for him to straighten the digits, but he waved his finger and said 'not possible.' A matronly nurse urged me into a wheelchair and we were taken to a ward with 'en-suite.'

Marie looked at me with disgust, anger and pity. We discussed how this might end our adventure, my career and our meagre savings. It crossed my mind that it may also end our marriage of 5 years.

The hospital room was spacious. My bed had a kapok pillow (no pillow case) and one sheet on a striped, stained, sagging mattress. Another small mattress was hauled in for Marie and left on the floor next to a trickling stream of water emanating from the cistern in the bathroom. Over night, we plotted our escape and come morning, we struggled to the front door en route to the wharf to hail the tender back to the *Socrates*.

But our plan was thwarted by the Matron, a nuggety woman, who wheeled us around like a rugby scrum and rucked us back to our room. She muttered something about payment. We feigned ignorance, replying 'no comprende.'

Breakfast consisted of white rice and liver, left over from the previous evening. At lunch time we received a visit from the *Socrates'* Venezuelan Shipping Agent. A young man fluent in

English. He agreed with us that the treatment was unsatisfactory and that we needed to relocate. Fortuitously, his father-in-law was an orthopaedic surgeon in the nearby regional capital of Valencia.

After satisfactory treatment in Valencia including straightening of the toes under local anaesthetic and a new plaster cast, we returned to the ship which had now berthed in the harbour. We were escorted to the Captain's office. He welcomed us back on board and asked if there was anything I needed. A new pair of crutches arrived the next day.

Two hours before sailing to our next port, two besuited men arrived on the ship. I was sure that they would detain us until health costs were settled. We were summoned to the Captain's cabin again. Surprisingly Señor Jimenez was with him. The Captain asked us how we were going to pay for the doctor, hospital and the crutches. I informed him that we were poor students and had no money to pay. Captain Van Dijk nodded in a fatherly, understanding way, but said nothing in reply.

'Cuanto?' The Señor asked the officious looking men. They produced an invoice which he quickly scanned, opened a manilla folder, extracted a bundle of his US dollars and began to count to $650.00. Looking up he then finalised the payment with 'Finito, eh?'

The men scooped up the cash, the Captain nodded and led us to the door. We had no time to thank the Señor properly. We watched as he walked down the gangplank towards his waiting car. He turned and waved, then tapped the side of his nose. I tapped my nose in response, the secret code now binding me into the Venezuelan Cartel.

When we left the ship in Cuidad Bolivar I asked the First Mate for our account so I could settle the Heineken bill. I was wary of the final sum, because I knew that my thirst for cheap beer in the humid Caribbean was probably 'over budget.' He returned with the Captain.

'The bill has already been paid Mr Williams. We all wish you and your wife a good trip from here.'

He nodded and raised his hand as if to give a naval salute. Instead, he tapped his nose, the salutation of the Cartel.

Our duplicitous acceptance of the Señor's largesse enabled us to finish our two month adventure backpacking around the countries of South America. We flew home from Santiago, Chile arriving in Sydney with $AUD10.00 – enough for train tickets to the Central Coast to stay with Marie's parents. I've never enjoyed a hot shower more, nor salivated as much over Joan's roast lamb dinner or slept as soundly in clean, fresh sheets.

In the ensuing weeks, Marie's pregnancy was confirmed and I learnt that I'd been appointed to Cardiff High School. We purchased a house in Arcadia Vale and Marie began casual teaching so we could try and replenish some savings. Todd was born in the tiny Rathmines Hospital, Lake Macquarie in September 1977. As a family we've since continued our travel adventures to weird and wonderful places.

We will never forget the MS *Socrates* and when I read of Pablo Escobar and the cocaine syndicates of South America, I think of Señor Jimenez and what a good bloke he was to two young, naive Aussies.

Faded Budgie Smugglers

Lap Nazis in tight low jammers demand lanes as they place
goggles, paddles, kick boards, fit-bits, pull buoys to claim territory.

Codgers totter the ramp to the briny
with jilted joints, scars and sagging skin.

Flamboyant femmes are splayed in scant thongs,
on oversized beach towels they preen and post selfies.

T-shirts and dank undies gape from faded sports bags
as retired men procrastinate, gossip and complain.

Young ladies flit and fiddle with straps, glasses, lip cream,
between photoing, posting and phubbing.

Tattooed Celtic bands encircle steroidal biceps
Maori designs on pakeha calves in cultural misappropriation.

Bogan gangs with mullets, sink rum and coke, drag ciggies,
blaspheme, expectorate and bombard in bum-crack boardies.

Classy ladies saunter, then recline with
glossed lips, lithe limbs, straw hats, dark polaroids.

Middle-aged men in desperation to thwart thickening waists
spar, stair climb and lap in faded budgie-smuggled hope.

Khayelitcha 1996

I'd been assured by Themba that it would be safe to go into Khayelitcha, South Africa's biggest township near Capetown. He'd contacted me after an article and photo in the *Cape Times* announced I was visiting the Medical Research Council to help establish school health education programs in the Province. As well as receiving nineteen letters from unemployed teachers wanting employment, I took a phone call from an earnest man wanting to be my assistant. He wanted to come to my office to meet me.

Themba was a qualified secondary teacher and a well dressed, good looking Xhosa man in his late twenties. He beseeched me to employ him because he was out of work and he had a wife and two young children to support. Unfortunately there were no funds to employ him.

After chatting and satisfying myself that Themba was a 'good bloke,' I accepted his offer to visit him at his home. He wanted to show me the township, no doubt because I would have empathy with him after being exposed to the hardships he and his wife faced there. I wanted to see first hand a South African slum, instead of forming an opinion as a gawking motorist speeding by.

We sped along the freeway across the dry, sandy flats north-east of Table Mountain and turned off onto a pot-holed, gravel road. Shanties of corrugated iron, concrete blocks, wood, cardboard and plastic sheeting engulfed us. The cool and constant sou'easter from the Atlantic stirred the dust and rolled the rubbish through the narrow laneways.

'We should at least be able to locate the hospital, we're supposed to meet Themba there.'

I confidently said to Todd, my 18 year old son as we slowly became disorientated and anxious of being absorbed by this alien place.

'There's a big brick building right over there,' Todd replied pointing to the far side across the hectares of mosaic huts.

We became locked in a maze of tiny streets and tracks, surrounded on all sides by humpies, leaking toilet blocks and small children. The residents peered at us in our little red hire car. We both immediately felt out of place as foreign privileged whites.

'But how do we get there? Jesus, Dad, do you know what you've got us in for?'

Two tall, striking, African adolescent boys walked towards us. Through my open window I asked if they could direct us to the hospital. They talked to each other in Xhosa before replying in impeccable English:

'We will show you,' and uninvited, they opened the back doors and jumped into the back seat.

I looked at Todd. He was pale, wide-eyed and his lips were parched. Had the kidnapping begun? I expected the blade of a knife to be put to either of our throats and ransom demands made followed by days in a bleak, cold concrete block. The thought was ill-founded because the boys were friendly, helpful and they asked for nothing. They guided us around a bitumen perimeter road to the Emergency Department. We shook their hands and thanked them. But we couldn't match their smiles which were as bright and as broad as I have ever seen.

'They were good young fellas,' I said to my son, hiding my own anxiety and trying to calm him. 'It's a nice introduction to a place that has a bad reputation.'

'Does anyone know we're here?' Todd's sensibilities tore at me.

'I think I mentioned it to my Head of Department,' I lied and looked ahead. Todd could read me like a book.

Nobody except Themba knew we were Australian and were not part of the former apartheid government although our accents may have indicated to our guides that we were different. We were blond, white males, no different in physical appearance to Afrikaners.

After locating our enthusiastic host he announced that we must gain approval from the African National Congress (ANC) to enter the township proper. I flinched because we had been convinced by first world media that the ANC were violent rebels who'd been trying for thirty years to overthrow the apartheid government. Todd looked at me with horror. I was terrified for us both but being a protective father I feared his demise more than mine.

Themba stode ahead leading us to a shipping container that served as the office. He explained that the ANC were like the local government for the township, and that we'd be OK as long as we had our passports. But his assurance didn't convince me. The plot was thickening, my anxiety was rising.

Upon entering the container I saw the large ANC flag, the black, green and yellow horizontal stripes wrapped around the shaft of a threatening spear. Call-to-action posters of pre-revolutionary times papered the steel walls. Photos of heroes like Nelson Mandela, Oliver Tambo and Steve Biko glared down from walls. A diagram of an AK 47 rifle was stuck to the side of a filing cabinet. A small air-conditioning unit rattled in a fruitless war against the humidity.

Then I saw the ANC representative behind the desk. His silent stern appearance was the most intense and intimidating that

I have ever encountered. His countenance was ice-cold and his clear, green eyes glared firmly from under his black, broad forehead as if he were looking straight through me. Two scars marked this young warrior's otherwise unblemished shiny face. One purple red blotch on his neck and a long scrape high on his cheek as if from a knife slash. He looked fit, powerful and menacing. He kept us standing, without a greeting, continuing his visual appraisal, before gesturing for us to sit in two plastic chairs. His offsider, another striking cool character stood behind us, which made me feel more threatened. After uncomfortable moments of silence he asked in a cool, calculated voice:

'Why are you here?'

Our host, Themba, began to hurriedly explain our bonafides. I nervously stumbled through an explanation emphasising how I would be helping children in disadvantaged schools, hoping to gain credit with this Xhosa chief.

He asked for our passports and in endless silence studied every page and every visa stamp. He glared at my tall, blonde, handsome boy after looking at his passport photo. It was not the brief glance of an immigration officer, but a glowering gawk as if assessing Todd's criminal intent.

I wiped my sweating palms across my thighs and looked at Todd. He took a swig from his water bottle to moisten his dry mouth. I questioned my parenting skills. Why would a father expose a vulnerable, loving, naive boy, fresh out of school to this experience? Maybe they would keep him and send me out to find the ransom? The idea filled me with dread.

Mr ANC handed the documents back, and nodded to Themba. It was a relief to be out of the dark cell and into the brilliant sunshine, buffeted by the cool wind. Shielding our eyes from the glare and dust we followed Themba on foot, leaving our car outside ANC headquarters.

As we walked along the sandy roads of the township, people came out of their homes to stare, inquisitive and puzzled by our presence. Around the bathroom blocks were puddles of dirty water. Skip bins overflowed with plastic and compostable rubbish, while the township's dogs scavenged for scraps. We dodged children playing soccer. We saw evidence of veggie patches, but the season was late summer and nothing would grow here without constant water and protection.

Mothers sitting on makeshift chairs nursed infants and chatted in communal conversation. Washing hung from wire strung between shacks. Women in colourful head wraps lent on brooms in the doorways of their abodes. Men congregated in small groups in whatever shade they could find peering suspiciously at us. Young people queued at the scarce public phone boxes.

Themba's small, square concrete block house was exceptionally clean and tidy. The four equal sized rooms were partitioned by unmatched cloth curtains. The small spaces contained worn and well-used furniture. Themba's wife had qualifications in law and worked three days a week in an attorney's office. They were making a go of it the best way they could manage. It was a raw, stark and confronting contrast between our quarter acre block, large house and green neighbourhood in suburban Newcastle.

As we retrieved our car, we noticed the ANC lieutenant monitoring us from the doorway of his office. I acknowledged him with a brief wave and nod of the head. He returned the gesture and watched us drive away, seeming pleased that the insurgents had left his patch.

'I think we'll go down to the Waterfront for a beer, mate. What do ya reckon?'

Errol

Errol's way was the opposite of mine. He nimbly climbed over the barbed wire fence down the back of the school and jumped balletically into the long paspalum below. Under his arm were a couple of dog-eared exercise books and a dirty pencil case. His blue school shirt hung out the back of an old pair of shorts that were too big for him. He then quickly disappeared into the corn paddock heading to his home across the river flat.

I'd never seen where he lived. My father told me he camped on the river bank along with many indigenous families who came to pick beans at Bega. That explained why Errol only stayed at school for a month or two and then he'd reappear the year after for the next bean crop.

My way home was via the front gate like all the other white kids. Our uniforms were intact, no buttons missing and I was sure to have my socks pulled up as protocol dictated, revealing my white knobbly knees below a pair of grey, serge shorts. Sometimes I waited under the Australian Flag to be picked up, otherwise I'd walk along the footpaths to my neat and tidy house.

In my Globite case were neatly covered school books, scrunched up jumper and the crusts of white bread from the Devon-and-tomato sauce sandwiches. I can never remember Errol having lunch. He'd sit on the bulbous roots of the peppercorn tree near the fence or when he got restless, throw stones at the fence posts. He was so accurate that we wouldn't play branding with him.

At playtime, Errol was always sure to take two bottles of free school milk. We were only allowed one each, but Errol guzzled his before any teacher could say anything. None of us kids dobbed him in for fear of being bashed. He won every playground fight, even against older kids.

He was a natural at sport – bigger, faster, stronger and was always the first picked in a make-up team before school or at lunch time. You just knew you'd lose if he was against you. He was a great teammate, be it cricket, footie or British bulldog. But Errol never got to do the picking. He was never nominated captain, but always told where he could play.

I wondered about Errol's house. Did he have a room like mine and a table with an electric light to do his homework? Where was his bike? Why wasn't he at Cubs? Who were his parents?

Sometimes we saw Errol on weekends in summer. Our swimming holes weren't that far from the 'Blacks' Camp' as my mother called it. We'd see the Aboriginal kids swing very high from a rope and then plunge into a deep hole. They were always more daring than us. Other times they lay back in the warm shallows like I did in the bath at home. But how did Errol wash and shower in winter? Did they have a toilet like us? I couldn't even see a long dropper. The women often washed clothes in the river and hung them on a makeshift line strung up between the she-oaks. We had a new Hills Hoist in the backyard.

In town, I'd see him with other Aborigines but we never spoke, just silently acknowledged each other with fleeting eye contact. I could never discern who his mother and father were because there were always quite a few adults with the kids. We were just Mum, Dad, Nanna, me and my brother.

When we were allowed to go to the pictures we always sat upstairs. I sometimes saw Errol and his mob, but they were always downstairs up the front. When the lights went out and the film rolled, some older kids used to throw Jaffas at the Aborigines. There was always a commotion and shouts of retribution from below.

One day, my best friend and I decided to venture down to the river to look at the camp. We knew someone was there because we could see blue smoke lazily curling up from a campfire. Darting behind the huge casuarina trunks we got close enough to see men sitting together smoking and women poking the fire to stoke a camp oven. We couldn't see power poles and wondered how they'd see at night without electricity. Their corrugated iron humpies and faded ex-army tents looked decrepit compared to our three-bedroom fibro house in a neat street in town. Errol's front yard was river sand, mine a manicured lawn. Some jalopies were abandoned along the sandy track. Maybe that explained why the blacks walked everywhere.

Errol disappeared after a few years. He never came to High School. But when I was sixteen, an Aboriginal man came up to me in the main street one Saturday morning.

'Hello Phillip,' he said, and looked me in the eye. 'Remember me, I'm Errol.' He held out his hand. We shook. I knew the name and was immediately taken back to my primary school days although I couldn't see the boy in the man who stood before me.

'Hello Errol, good to see you. How are you going?'

The person in front of me was an adult. I was a pimply-faced teenager in shorts and long socks. I was surprised that he remembered me at all. Errol fondly recalled the days when we played together at school.

'I'm livin' up in Nowra now. We're down here pickin' the beans again. It's always good to come back to Bega. You still at school? You been goin' good at swimmin' eh?'

The question-and-answer conversation was brief. Why was it so hard for me to not feel a closer connection? Why didn't I try to stay in touch? I wish that I had. I've missed so much.

We wandered off to our own worlds.

Postscript

Now, 53 years later I mourn that I never made an effort to befriend Errol as I did with my white mates. I treated him as different, like all white kids did. He lived separately, not part of us. I had no regard for him or his family; no inkling of his heritage. We weren't taught about Indigenous history or culture at school, only the early explorers and white settler families of the Valley.

We were, and still are, ignorant of the Bega Valley tribes, their interactions, sacred sites, culture and their environment. The First Nations people of Australia were innocent victims of colonisation and have been diminished. In a way, I played an innocent part in that process. I regret missing the opportunity to befriend Errol and learn about his way of life and the challenges he faced.

Lines of Steel

Graham clip-clopped into the kitchen after his morning ride along the Fernleigh Track when his phone pinged.

'G, yet another bloke has come off his bike after getting caught in the tram tracks broke his leg and shoulder. We're organising a protest to have a bike lane put in. Next sat at 10.30am Pacific Park See you there.'

Graham was wearing his bright Lycra top, tight cycling shorts and wrap around sunnies. His wife Gwendolyn had tried to convince him that he looked ridiculous dressed like that, with his pot belly and protruding love handles. She didn't know how the tiny little racing bike held his ample weight.

Graham showed her the message.

'There was a photo in *The Herald* the other day of a worker filling in the tram tracks on Scott Street so the Supercars could go across smoothly,' Gwen said.

'That'd be right, wouldn't it. They'd do anythin' for the bloody Supercars and nothing for the bike riders. You can't even ride or walk through Newcastle East for weeks while those V8s suck the life out of the town. It's a bloody disgrace what's goin' on.'

'Here we go again,' Gwen mused.

'That's the Guv'ment for ya. They promised there'd be a bike lane but no – its just for cars and that bloody useless light rail. Them tram tracks are a death trap for bike riders up the East End.'

'You know, my old Pop used to ride over a lot of railway lines riding to work at the BHP. There were hundreds who rode bikes back in those days. No one ever complained or fell off,' Gwen countered.

'Yeah, but their bikes had big tyres back then, so they couldn't get stuck. Bikes are different now.'

'Why is that the Government's fault?' she asked.

'For Christ's sake Gwen, don't start!'

Graham didn't want a debate with his wife of 37 years about the rights of cyclists. Since retiring he'd become an avid rider. His whole life seemed to revolve around bikes and injuries from mishaps.

'Why do you have to ride where the tram lines are anyway, when you can go another way? Why do people put themselves in those positions? You'd think the cyclists would know better.'

Gwen took a tea towel and busied herself at the sink.

Graham poured a cup of tea and sliced some bread for the toaster.

'The Government want people to get off their arses and lose weight, yet they make it hard for us. There's no consideration of ordinary people like us. Who's gunna use the tram anyway? It's a folly and a big waste of money.'

'All I'm saying is, that Pop rode across lines of steel and never fell off once in thirty years. So what's the difference? He rode in his work clothes and no helmet. They weren't lit up like a Christmas trees in Lycra either,' Gwen fired back.

'The laws are different now. You have to wear a helmet or you get fined. And everyone wears cycling gear. It's what you do when you ride a bike.'

'Those new tram tracks would have been made by BHP if they were still operating you know.' Gwen reminisced, taking the chance to lament BHP's closure .

'Who knows where they've come from, probably China. The tram's been made in Spain for God's sake! They could have been made here in Cardiff! That's the Guv'ment for ya.' Graham repeated his mantra.

'Pop and his mates liked to ride to work because it meant they could get across the hill and down to the Stag and Hunter for a few beers after work before the rush. They'd just lean their bikes against the pub wall. They didn't lock 'em. Everyone knew each other's bike. Then they'd ride home three parts to the wind drunk. But they never got caught in the tracks like they seem to be doin' now.'

'Barry had his new bike taken last week in the mall. He took his eye off it for 30 seconds while he ordered coffee. When he looked around it was gone. No sign of it since. Paid over seven grand for it, fully imported, lightweight carbon fibre frame.'

Graham wanted to change the focus of the conversation as he smeared Vegemite on the toast.

'Why would you pay that much for a bicycle? He already had a good one you said.'

Graham shrugged. He hadn't told Gwen that his bike had cost him five thousand.

'Pop and his mates had Malvern Stars. All made in Australia from good BHP steel. Backpedal brakes, mud-guards and no gears. His was red because he reckoned it would go faster. It was in his shed when he died you know? He had it all his life. Used to give us a double on the handlebars when we were kids.'

Graham had heard this story, and many more, about Gwen's grandfather. He let her talk while he ate his breakfast. The words washed over him.

The following Saturday Graham rode into town to the Pacific Park protest. He told Gwen there could be up to one thousand bike riders who planned to ride all the way along Scott and

Hunter Street. He kissed her on the cheek and told her that he'd be home for lunch.

After grocery shopping and cleaning, Gwen was preparing sandwiches when her mobile rang. She did not recognise the number so she didn't answer.

A few minutes later, she heard the ping of the message app.

'Gwen, this is Barry, one of Graham's cycling mates. He's had a fall. The ambos took him to John Hunter unconscious. Didn't have his helmet on. Got caught in the lines of steel. Looks like concussion, dislocated collar bone and lots of bark off his legs. He brought down seven others with him. Please ring.'

Maria Magic

A three-night yoga retreat on Maria Island off the east coast of Tasmania is not everyone's cup of tea, especially for a non-yogi like me. But I was persuaded to tag along. On the first night we met the others, 15 female yogis and Suzie, our leader, yoga master and cook. She is a tall, strong and charismatic woman. Her grace, organisational skill and knowledge impressed us. We sat around one big table in the community kitchen. It allowed us to chat and get to know each other before we were invited to the Chapel for a short yoga session.

Afterwards we bedded down in our sleeping bags in room 9 of the penitentiary. There were three double bunks on either side of the large, bare, cold room. Theresa from St Kilda took the top bunk near the small window. I was in the bottom bunk near the door. Marie lay on the bottom bunk in the middle. It had been a long day after an early morning flight from Sydney to Hobart, a drive to the small fishing town of Triabunna and a forty minute ferry ride across Mercury Passage.

I lay back and thought about the interesting women I'd met in the past few hours. They were wise, resourceful and creative. There was a quiet energy about this group. As the only male, I find it hard to describe, but there was something that told me this weekend was going to be very different. Maria Island meant a lot to many of the women, especially Suzie. Some had described a strong incentive to attend because it was being held on the Island. The weekend's activities provided an opportunity for them to 'reset' from their busy lives at home, to rest and enjoy each other's company.

Sleep descended quickly but I was woken by a strange sensation on my the chest. I was startled and scared because I thought it was the big Tasmanian possum that had interrupted our yoga earlier in the evening. As my eyes adjusted in the moonlit room a tiny man with his legs astride my sternum came into focus. He was dressed in an old fashioned French Naval Uniform and appeared like an animated porcelain doll stamping his feet to get my full attention. Dark irises peered from under the high naval hat brim. A deep and powerful accented voice boomed as through a speaking trumpet.

'I saw you in the quadrangle with the wombats an hour ago' he said. 'I want to know what you're doing here!'

'Who are you?' I whispered, so as not to wake the others. Was this spectre here to enforce French colonial power, I wondered? Why was he so demanding?

'Why are you whispering?' he demanded.

'Because we are practising Mouna or silence for 12 hours. It's part of this weekend's yoga.'

He frowned and shook his little head from side to side, clearly not understanding.

'In Yoga practice, silence is god, power, the very force and purpose of our existence.'

'My name is Rene Mauge de Cely and I am a French Zoologist. I am part of Captain Baudin's crew of Le Geographe. I am 42 yrs old and have been interred on Maria Island since 1802 as I died from dysentery while anchored in Oyster Bay. Since my death and burial I've been keeping an eye on happenings for my eventual report to Napoleon Bonaparte.'

Was I dreaming? How could this perfect little man on my chest be looking directly into my eyes and communicating with me so clearly? His clean crisp uniform was perfect, everything was in place. Moonlight beams highlighted the rich gold braid on his long, navy blue coat. He looked proud and strong with his brass buttons and striped epaulets. The high collar was spectacular and his white pantaloons looked as though they'd just been washed and pressed.

'Why are you in Officer's uniform?' I asked.

'Because I was given that status due to my professional standing as one of the team of zoologists on the expedition. We are to report on botanical and faunal specimens and on the indigenous inhabitants of Van Dieman's Land.'

'Who was Van Dieman?' I questioned, showing my vast ignorance.

'Anthony Van Dieman was the Governor General of the Dutch East India Company in Batavia when Abel Tasman, the famous Dutch explorer discovered this land in 1642. He also named this place 'Maria's Eylandt' after Van Dieman's wife.'

'You said Mareeeya not Mariiiah.' I was confused about how to pronounce Maria.

'It was Mareeya,' he responded, 'but sometime ago it became Mariiiah, probably because the British changed it, as they did to most things just to suit themselves. Ever since they came here I've been watching what they've been doing and the trouble they've created. They claimed the land as their own. That was their intention from the very beginning, unlike us who came here for science. We didn't even camp on the land. We always returned to our boats in the evening to sleep so the indigenous people felt no threat of invasion or theft of land.

'The English have since decimated the aborigines here. They cleared the land for farming, introduced sheep, cattle and pests including cats. They've brought prisoners here, a cruel and criminal act in my view. Not to mention their treatment of these so-called convicts. The English are imperialist bullies who deserve to be put back on their little island so the rest of us can create a civilised world.'

I tried to recall the geopolitical events in Europe at the end of the C18th, the rise of Napoleon and the threat he posed to England.

'Now sir, may I call you Philippe?' I nodded my assent to be on first name terms.

'Philippe, I am one of just a few 'historical custodians' of this special place and I would like to introduce you to another, Bara-Oura.'

He held out his arm across my chest towards the side of the bed.

'Come, s'il nous plait. Don't be nervous. Philippe is a good man.'

I sensed some light pressure on my ribs and then saw a young aboriginal woman hold her hand out to grasp the Monsieur's. As she came closer I could clearly see her white teeth, her eyes and the beautiful, thick possum skin cloak she wore around her body. She was taller than the Monsieur with long lean legs and arms. She had short hair in the manner of today's closely cropped spiked hairdos of some women.

'Bara-Oura is quite shy, unlike me, but she wants to tell her story, like we all do, about the Island.'

'I came to wukaluwikiwayna with two girl friends from my pukikwilayte family group in 1802. We crossed Oyster Bay in our big bark and reed canoe on a calm day to collect food and to continue the culture that our mothers and grandmothers had taught us. We sat in the rear with our four men paddling at the front. We had our dogs and spears for the men to hunt wallaby, possum and wombats.'

I strained to hear her soft and gentle voice but nodded to let her know that I understood and wanted to know more. I was engrossed in the beauty of Bara-Oura. I felt that it was just the beginning of a long, fascinating journey for me.

'We brought our baskets with stone tools to dig out the red and white ochre from the Painted Rocks. I liked to dive for shell-fish and I used my dilly bag around my neck so I had a place to put oysters and scallops as I collected.'

Monsieur Mauge was listening intently too and he nodded again for Bara-Oura to continue.

'I can remember watching my friends on the beach, their bodies stooped, heads bent, gently sweeping the sands with their hands for the little shells. Our grandmothers taught us. Other times we would spend days searching through the wet, stinky seaweed seeking out tinier shells. Sometimes we searched the creeks to look for the really brilliant green snail shells.'

Then I noticed her necklaces. They were stunning. Intricate and beautiful with larger green shells spaced between the tiny white shells. One necklace was tight around her neck. The other hung lower across her chest.

'This one was given to me by my grandmother,' she said as she lifted the longer, looser necklace toward me so that I could see more clearly.

Her face softened and I saw some mistiness in her eyes. I felt very sad about seeing this proud young woman talking with me and to realise what had happened 150–200 years ago. It also occurred to me that Bara-Oura and her friends were the 'cultural jewellers' of their tribe. The strings of shells would be handed down, generation to generation to become an important part of their cultural heritage.

Was there any connection between this weekend's yoga pilgrimage and that of Bara-Oura's over 200 years earlier. Women were coming together for companionship. Was it an unseen and unspoken link to the indigenous women of Van Dieman's Land?

Suzie had recognised some type of connection because she had spoken in the evening yoga session of the original inhabitants and how we need to be mindful of their presence and of their ancestors.

Bara-Oura spoke again.

'One morning we saw a small floating island with two, three, very tall trees; this strange island – it crept up on us in the night. We did not know what it was; it frightened us, we all ran away. Later I learned it was a ship. It was the first ship to come to my homeland wukaluwikiwayna.'

'That was my ship, Le Geographe, commanded by Nicholas Baudin,' Monsieur Mauge proudly said, cutting off Bara-Ora. In text book fashion Rene went on.

'On board we had a team of French scientists – naturalists, botanists, zoologists, illustrators and teams of assistants. Napoleon Bonaparte signed his approval for France's 'Voyage of Discovery to the Southern Lands' and the ships sailed out of the Port de Le Havre on 19 October 1800 to great fanfare. Le Geographe was accompanied by a support ship Le Naturaliste, captained by Jacques Hamelin.'

'Why are you here with a group of 15 women; why were you all in the other room lying on mats doing unusual exercises; who is the woman with the curly hair who sits at the front and sings 'Om' at the finish?' he demanded.

Before I could answer they were both gone. They must have been scared off by Marie's sleepy murmurings and movement in the next bunk. I stayed awake for quite some time thinking about my encounter with Monsieur Mauge and Bara-Oura wondering if it was true and what it all meant.

Then Suzie's 'call-to yoga' bells rang quaintly outside the door. It was 5.15am.

I told no-one about my encounter, considering it a dream.

But somehow, I knew differently. Because on Saturday night Monsieur Mauge was back, and he was with another 'historical custodian'.

'Bon nuit Philippe' he greeted me. 'This is my colleague and friend William Smith O'Brien. William was sent here as a convict – a political prisoner to be precise. He was sentenced to be hanged, drawn and quartered in England simply because he wanted independence for his own people and land.'

William greeted me with a warm smile and he outstretched his tiny arm in a hand shake gesture. I touched his hand with my index finger. William spoke in a strong Irish brogue and was not quite as tall as the Frenchman. Like Monsieur Mauge, he was dressed immaculately in a brown suit, white shirt, black tie and vest, elastic sided black polished boots and he wore an Irish design herringbone cap.

'Can you talk with us or are you still...,' he raised his little hands and with his fingers and made gestures like apostrophes 'In touch with God through silence?'

'I can talk with you, even though we are doing the Mouna again.'

I didn't want to miss the incredible experience I was having with these two impressive historical characters and there was no consequence for talking during Mouna. Suzie had told us we would not be struck down by a Yoga god.

'I'm pleased to meet you Mr Smith,' I said, as I propped myself up slightly out of the sleeping bag without upsetting the mens' balance on my chest.

Monsieur Mauge continued.

'Philippe, please call me Rene and him William,' he said as he pointed to his Irish colleague. 'We're all on first name terms here because we're all opposed to English hegemony aren't we Philippe? Especially as an Australian, you'd be anti-British because the Brits still consider you all to be inferior convict stock.'

'I'm with you because we are still striving to become a Republic with an Australian Head of State. So please tell me why you are here?' I asked the Irish gentleman.

'I was brought here as a political prisoner in 1825 as one of 50 men on the Prince Leopold. I was an Irish Nationalist Member of Parliament and convicted of sedition.'

This seemed like a well rehearsed speech and he was delivering it with great aplomb, emphases and hand movements.

'I was seen as a threat because of my political views. My death sentence was commuted to exile in Van Dieman's Land. I was given a vegetable patch to work and was not allowed to speak to anyone. Even here on Maria Island they were worried that I could undermine them. That's when Rene came into my life and we've been friends ever since. Now we're both working against the system to overthrow tyranny.'

He threw his fist into the air and stamped his 'big' little boot into my chest. I was impressed with his commitment after all this time.

The lilt of his Irish accent intrigued me. It was such a mellifluous, flow of words that I thought I could listen all day. And as he spoke his neatly trimmed moustache rose and fell with each tone and beat. I was captured by him and I could easily understand how his speeches could arouse passion with empathic followers.

'Philippe, why were you all walking in a line, very slowly this morning along the track? It looked to me like a convict work line going to fell trees.' Rene asked, changing the subject.

'Oh, that was walking meditation. We walk slowly and take in all the sights, sounds and smells of what's around us. It's to help centre us and prepare us for the day.'

'We have seen the woman who leads your group on the island many times,' William said.

'We like her because she looks strong, independent and resourceful. And we've noticed that she prepares all the food and organises the whole group for the day. The food you are eating is new to us. We've smelt the aromas and flavours emanating from her pots. She uses spices and herbs that are not normally found here. We've tried to open her big food boxes during the night to eat some of it but we don't have the strength.'

'Well, Suzie is a remarkable person and you should meet her if you get the chance. She is committed to restoring the natural environment on the Island. She volunteers to work with National Parks in planting indigenous trees and shrubs to areas that were cleared. I'm sure her views are similar to yours. You could recruit her to your cause,' I said.

By the time I'd finished speaking my little friends had gone. Then I heard the soft tinkle of Suzie's bell. It was 5.30am and the sun was not yet up. But already Theresa and Marie were dressing, in silence, for yoga.

I found it hard to relax in the Yoga meditation pose because of my clandestine meeting during the night. I was determined to come back to Maria Island, for a longer time so I could reconnect with Bara-oura, Rene and William and learn more about them, how they live and about the history of the Island.

I'd like to know more about the Indigenous people of the area and if they were murdered as part of the 'Black Line' policy in 1830 or were they 'rounded up' and shipped to Flinders Island with aborigines from other parts of Tasmania?

What was the full story of the 'charming, persuasive, loquacious and daring' Diego Bernacchi, an Italian, who with an 'irrepressible urge,' was granted land on the island to establish sericulture (silk) and viticulture industries? How good was his

Maria Island wine that won recognition at the Melbourne Centennial Exhibition?

How did the timber getters transport their logs from the island to their mills on the coast?

How productive was the cement works that mined the limestone from fossilised shells in the cliffs near the Darlington township? Why hasn't the parent company removed its huge, ugly concrete silos and other buildings from the Island?

What did the historical custodians think of the small cruise ships that now anchor in the bay and bring their hordes to the jetty in small boats?

Where do the 'day-trippers' come from? Those tourists who catch the ferry in the morning, walk to the convict buildings, take photos and return to the wharf a few hours later?

What do they think of photographs and how would my small friends know about selfie sticks and the thousands of photos on Facebook and Instagram of selected parts of Maria Island?

Will my three new, proud and formidable comrades in their perfect C19th dress remember me?

I hope so, because I will always remember them.

Will Bara-Oura, Rene and William talk with Suzie?

I hope so, because they would make a powerful team.

Postscript

The Museum d'historie naturelle in Le Havre holds more than 1500 drawings (including 150 engravings), 1400 manuscripts and almost 3000 documents connected with the voyage of Discovery in the years 1800–1804. Their number alone serves to demonstrate what an extraordinary undertaking this voyage was.

Nicholas Baudin died on the return journey to France in Mauritius on 16 September 1803 from dysentery.

Point Mauge on Maria Island was named after Baudin's friend and colleague, Rene Mauge de Cely. Rene was buried there on 21 February 1802.

William Smith O'Brien attempted to escape Maria Island on board a ship. But the master of the schooner hired to bring Smith to freedom betrayed him and he was sent to Port Arthur. He later returned to the UK and became one of the leaders of the Young Ireland Movement and the failed Rebellion in 1848. He died in Wales in 1864.

Monica and Michael

'It's criminal to leave me out here, abandoned in this overgrown backyard. Since they dumped me, I've felt frail, vulnerable and depressed. I miss my friends and I miss Michael. He was so good to me. There's no-one to talk to here. I'm so lonely. The only thing that keeps me going are the memories I have as a clothes dummy. I was useful. There were customers. I was important. We would chat.

My funnest job was at the costume hire shop when I was dressed as Morticia from the Addams Family. I attracted a lot of attention. Some brazen customers would reposition me right up close to Uncle Fester as if we were lovers. It was a bit embarrassing, but I secretly liked being near someone. It gave me a sense of security. You know, just being close.

And then there were the superheroes like Wonder Woman. Being in disguise made me feel cheeky and strong, as if I was immortal. I attracted some attention I can tell you! Especially from children. And then there were always some pathetic men who'd pinch and grope me. Easy way for them to get some cheap kicks.

Before then I was at David Jones as their top clotheshorse in the Hunter Street store. I came up from Sydney after being specially made. They wanted to capitalise on the Twiggy fashion craze. You know, when Jean Shrimpton appeared in her mini skirt at the Flemington races back in the 1960's. 'Tall, thin, sexy, long legs,' was the brief DJ's gave to the dummy manufacturer. I was front and centre of their main window for two decades. I felt good to be the only bespoke dummy.

I have such good memories of being there. Michael was the head window dresser and he took a special interest in me. Talked to me all the time while he was fitting me with new outfits. He was very attentive and wanted everything perfect. He was a small, neat man who'd never married. Told me he had been with DJ's since he was 16 years old. He always wore a suit with a bright pocket handkerchief, a different one every day of the week. And a bow tie to match. He looked quite the part. We were almost family.

When Mike left DJ's, he tried to buy me, but they said no, I was going on to further my modelling career elsewhere. He could have kept in touch I'm sure. Maybe he found someone new, one of those metrosexual models they have now? Someone else to tell they 'were the most beautiful mannequin I've ever worked with.'

But since I was sold and went to that dreadful place in the Hunter Valley, I've not seen hide nor hair of him. The new owners put me out on the footpath, for God's sake. Dressed me in 'the specials' – cheap, gaudy clothes. Once in winter, I was put in a maroon chenille dressing gown and slippers! A woman like me! The hide of them!

That was where I lost my arm. Some school kids knocked me over. Shook me up quite a bit. The owners said they couldn't fix me. I'll never forgive them, but what could I do?

And here I am now – weatherbeaten, cold and lonely with grass growing around my legs. The backyard is full of broken things. Mr Victa Mower is my constant companion. I talk, he listens. He's got nothing to say, typical male, but it's nice that he's near. Sleeps most of the time. He's useless, but I lean on him and he gets an eyeful all day because they've given me no proper clothes unless the kids dress me up.

It's shocking what happens to old dummies like me these days, discarded and forgotten. When I think about all the dummies DJ's had, I wonder where they've gone? We all got on so well. Like one big family. Now we're separated. They're probably locked away in homes or granny flats waiting to pass. Out of sight – out of mind. Seems to be happening more and more to older folks like me.

The past three years have been the worst. Except for those afternoons when Dipti and Ravi pop through the fence. Little Dipti dresses me up in bright saris and the silk feels so nice against my peeling skin. She put the sunglasses on me because she said I had wrinkles. Cheeky little devil.

Ssshh! listen, someone's coming! Can you believe it? I hear the gate dragging open and footsteps coming down the driveway.

Oh My Gosh! It's Michael. He's standing in front of me. I want to hug him. I hear his wonderful calm voice. I feel warm, excited and so relieved.'

'Hello Monica. I've missed you very much. It's taken such a long time to find you. You're still beautiful. You're coming home with me now. We'll get you fixed up in no time. New arm, nice clothes and a comfortable position in my sunroom near the sewing machine. I'll look after you. It'll be just like old times.You and me together. Be good to catch up on what you've been doing.'

The Blueberry Tales

Jason's Uber passengers were mostly the old dears he ferried home from Woolies on pension day. Then there were regulars from the Coffs Harbour RSL Club after Friday night footy. Sometimes requests came from teenagers heading off to parties at the beach. Jason knew most of them. They were good kids and they treated Jason like a friendly uncle. But the pick-up address on his screen was unfamiliar as he checked the Uber App message at 7.30am. According to Google Maps, the residence was at the end of a dead-end road about 15 km out of town. Uber had calculated a fare of $45.50 which was a good one to have compared to the piddling $10 or $12 fares, minus the Uber fee from the locals.

Jason slurped down his coffee, checked on his Dad and grabbed the keys. He pointed the Camry north on the Pacific Highway before turning left towards the mountains. The last time he'd been out this way was on a school excursion in Year 11 to study the biodiversity of the rainforest. That was 12 years ago before he dropped out of school. Chasing waves and girls up and down the coast instead of studying for HSC was not the best life choice he'd ever made.

Now, there was no rainforest except in the deep gullies. The tall trees, gurgling creeks and bountiful birds had been replaced with blueberry plantations. A monoculture of neatness, order and control. It was the exact opposite of what nature intended for this land. The parallel lines of tall bushes spanned hectare after hectare, much of it protected by white plastic netting to repel hail and to keep birds from feeding off the crop.

161

Jason was appalled because his Dad, Malcolm, had been a State Forester before his accident. He'd taught his son the value of the bush as a living ecosystem. Jason wasn't a 'greenie' in a fundamentalist way, but he was a Greens voter and could hold his own in any debate about the importance of environmental conservation. His dear dad lamented the destruction of 'magical, irreplaceable North Coast rainforest by clear felling for urban development and bloody blueberries!'

The sprawling white mansion up on the ridge came into view before Google indicated the next turn left. Jason slowed the Camry to reduce the dust on the approach to the McMansion, then came to a halt on the crunchy red scoria at the bottom of the stairs. The patio was adorned with large pots of golden and burnt orange marigolds that offset perfectly the glare from the white marbled facade. Two black Mercedes SUVs were in the open garage.

A slim, tall young man walked across the patio carrying a leather briefcase. Jason's eyes widened at the red turban, pressed trousers and collared white shirt. He'd never had an Indian passenger in his car. He immediately regretted 'under-dressing' as he glanced down at his torn jeans, CAT work boots and black AC/DC T-shirt.

'G'day there.' Jason welcomed him through the window noting that the passenger was looking at the wheelchair hoist on the car roof.

'Hello. My name is Ravi. I'm going to Grafton please.'

Ravi turned and waved to the older woman standing by the front door. Her jet black hair was pulled back into a plait and she wore a loose fitting pantsuit. Ravi's Mum, thought Jason.

'But Uber tells me you're going to Coffs train station?'

'Not now, sorry. My business has been transferred, and besides, I'm running late. Can you do it? I'll give you cash.'

'Sure can.'

Jason loved the chance to earn cold hard cash. Anything to keep the dollars away from Uber. But why wasn't this smart young Indian guy driving himself?

'How late are ya? What time's your appointment?' Jason asked Ravi.

'I need to be at the Court House at 11.15.'

'By the way, my name's Jason.'

The mental arithmetic for the trip duration didn't quite add up because he needed fuel at the Woolgoolga Ampol and that meant driving well over the speed limit. And how much to charge him?

As the Camry pulled away from house and back down the slopes to the Highway, Jason, ever talkative, kick-started the conversation. There was so much to know.

'Love the turban. Looks *so* cool!'

'My father prefers me to wear the turban when I'm representing the family company. He believes it helps create a respectful ambience for business negotiations.'

Jason nodded, noting the formal tone of Ravi's response and now regretted the crude way that he'd commented on his turban. His father had urged him to be more tactful, to think before speaking. But Jason found it a stretch because he had such infectious enthusiasm for all things in life.

'And what about you Jason? Is driving an Uber your business?'

'It's my car, but I only do it when it suits, about three or four days a week. I live with my dad who's disabled and he takes a lot of my time. I sometimes help out a friend who owns a long-haul trucking business. I drive forklifts and move pallets and containers in his yard early some mornings. I've got a heavy vehicle licence. Just love drivin' – you know? But I can't do long hauls since dad had his accident. I'm his primary carer and need to be around for him.'

Ravi, nodding, did not respond but stared ahead seemingly lost in thought.

'I'm sorry to hear that. You drive very well Jason. I feel safe with you, thank you.'

He clicked on the cruise control at 115kph, knowing that it was the upper limit of tolerance for the highway patrol. Jason knew a lot of the coppers and they knew his car, so he reckoned his speed would be sweet to make Grafton in time for his very likeable new customer.

'And your business is blueberries I take it?'

Jason wanted to know more about the mid-north coast Indian community that had created such a huge and profitable berry industry. Some of his surfer mates hated the Indians claiming that they'd taken over Woolgoolga, infiltrated the schools and ripped off the seasonal workers who picked the berries. None of them liked their ugly Sikh Temple on the highway despite being partial to the spicy Indian takeaways after a morning surf.

'My family owns four blueberry farms. My grandfather and his brothers migrated here in the 1960s from the Punjab and found work with local banana growers. They slowly made money, bought their own farms and planted blueberries. Others followed and we are now the biggest region for blueberries in Australia.'

Ravi recited this information as if he had said it many times over. It seemed like a rehearsed monotone. Jason wondered how happy he was. Did he have friends? A relationship?

'My parents sent me to a private school in Brisbane and now I'm studying for an MBA at Bond. I'm destined to take over the business.'

Jason detected no enthusiasm in Ravi's voice, it was more a statement of resignation, as if his family had mapped out a life for him. Apart from his dad, Jason had no siblings and only a couple of much older distant cousins. His mum was in WA, having left her paralysed husband and son for a younger man in Margaret River.

They arrived at the Court House with three minutes to spare.

'Text me when you're ready mate, and good luck in there.' Jason gave him a thumbs-up and then watched Ravi climb the steps up to the imposing Court House.

❖

After picking up a takeaway coffee he drove to a quiet riverside park to await the return journey. The Clarence was swollen with floodwaters. White patches of spume swirled on the surface like froth on a chocolate milkshake. Sticks, logs and small trees raced towards Yamba and a final resting place on one of the North Coast beaches.

Jason dozed and listened to the calming susurration of the river, marvelling at the huge volume of water passing by every minute. His mind wandered to the sound of the gushing waterfalls within the rainforest where his father had taken him as a child. He recalled the dank smell of moss and lichen, the pungent odour of crushed leaves from a thin-leafed peppermint and the cool, pristine air that made his lungs yearn for more.

Malcolm had taught him how to scoop running water from a creek into his cupped hands and to slurp the cold liquid into his warm mouth. Jason had also learnt how to hug a forest giant by reaching around the trunk and looking up and marvelling at the complex canopy of its white branches and grey-green leaves. How he loved the evocative names of the eucalypts like flooded gum, blackbutt and brush box. It was an exhilarating feeling and made the young Jason feel that he was being treated to something that kids from the city would never experience.

When the accident happened, Malcolm had been in the bush alone and so absorbed in surveying the canopy wildlife that he tumbled backwards down a rocky slope cracking two vertebrae and fracturing his skull. Jason clearly remembers the day it happened eight years ago. His strong healthy dad has been unable to walk since, and was now confined to a wheel chair with paraplegia.

◈

'How did you go at court?' Jason asked when Ravi slid into the passenger seat at 12.45pm.

'Let's talk over lunch. I'm hungry. Go up the main street and we'll eat at my uncle's restaurant.'

Jason was delighted. 'I just love Indian food and so does my Dad. We get takeaway at least twice a week.'

Ravi's uncle served a lunch of samosas, paneer tikka and tandoori chicken with ice-cold cans of Pepsi. After a few mouthfuls of the delicious food, washed down with cola, Ravi's tongue began to loosen.

'Our blueberry businesses have caused environmental damage. It is a cause of great shame to me and to my extended family. In efforts to maximise profits we have clear-felled hectare after hectare causing massive erosion and topsoil run-off into local creeks. It's been a major factor contributing to flooding and has impacted on sea life and fishing.'

Jason was listening and nodding as he ripped the naan into pieces and dipped it into the tikka sauce. He'd read snippets in the Coffs Harbour Advocate.

'Isn't there something to do with fertiliser too?'

'In our efforts to grow more and bigger blueberries we have

over-used nitrogen to such an extent that it has damaged many parts of the ecosystem. It also means that we have wasted lots of money on fertiliser that has literally been washed away and those chemicals have impacted the reef too.'

Ravi's resignation and dejection was palpable.

'So what we've been doing is totally unsustainable. We've had compliance orders issued against us and impending fines, unless we change. That's the purpose of the trip and...' he paused 'my father wants me to take over this mess!'

'That's a big responsibility Ravi. Is it what you want to do?'

'My grandparents and my parents are poorly educated people. They came to Australia for a new life and to work hard for their families. Where they came from in the Punjab, there were no laws regulating the environment. They had no intention of violating legislation here. They just didn't know! All my uncles and their families are very sad that they are in trouble. They desperately want to fix the problems and restore their good reputation in the community. I have a responsibility to them.'

'Is this why you had to come to court?'

Ravi pushed back from the table, shook hands with his Uncle and walked to the door. He held it open for Jason. It was the first time anybody had held a door open for him.

'I'll fix up the bill,' offered Jason.

'No, there's no need. Really. It's all in the family.' Ravi smiled showing his perfect white teeth.

As they set off for the return trip, Ravi handed Jason five $50 notes.

'Will this cover your petrol and time Jason?'

'Yes, but it's way too much Ravi. One hundred is plenty.'

'No, no. You paid $72.55 for petrol at Woolgoolga. I will cover this cost for you and the rest is your wage for the day.' Ravi was now acting as his benevolent boss. Jason didn't mind, considering he'd eaten a great lunch as well.

The following Wednesday night, Jason received a text from Ravi.

Hi Jason, can you come to work at our farm tomorrow morning please. Our forklift driver has COVID, yet we have to load eight pallets of berries for Sydney markets. The long haul truck arrives around 7am. Please advise of your availability? Ravi

Jason replied:

See you at 6.45am Ravi. J

❖

After loading the pallets, Jason enjoyed the syrupy, spongy, deep-fried doughy sweets served by three young Indian women in the packing shed's cramped kitchen.

'My name is Sirika, I'm Ravi's big sister. Thank you for coming today and helping us. I hope you enjoyed the Gulab Jamun. It's a good sweet to have after working hard.'

Sirika's smile and charm disarmed Jason. Since leaving school he'd had two girlfriends, but the relationships had been short-lived. He found many Aussie girls smothering, demanding and totally addicted to social media. But Sirika was beautiful, peaceful and happy. There was not a mobile phone in sight. She seemed pleasantly different and Jason felt relaxed and accepted in her presence.

Ravi slipped from the shadow of the big shed into the brightly lit kitchen, offering Jason a white envelope.

'Thank you Jason. Do you mind cash? Everyone here appreciates you coming at very short notice. Would you be interested in doing more casual work if the opportunity arose?'

'Of course I would. You've got my number. I like it here Ravi. Anytime mate.'

❖

'Jason, can you please drive me to Sydney on Thursday? I have a meeting at 9.00am Friday. I'll arrange accommodation for you.'

'No worries Ravi. What time to leave?

Jason reversed the SUV out of the garage, excited to be driving such a luxury car.

'You look nice today,' Ravi said with a smile as he slid into the driver's seat. It was the first compliment Jason had received in a long time and he felt his neck redden as the warm flush of embarrassment spread across his face. He'd chosen his best clothes for the trip. A bold new check shirt from Rivers, a pair of cream chinos and elastic-sided brown boots that his father insisted he polish before leaving home, completing the ensemble.

As they passed the packing shed, he noticed Sirika waving from the doorway. He was unsure if she was waving to him, or Ravi, but he waved back anyway. Her broad smile captivated him.

Ravi wasted no time opening his iPad and tapped away, comfortable in his mobile office, travelling south on the M1. He took a phone call on speaker from his cousin, now a State MP who told him that there was to be a significant increase in the Environmental Levy imposed by the State Government. Growers would be required to enter into agreements with Southern Cross University to undertake remediation projects such as bush regeneration, erosion control and something called 'surface-flow bioreactors.'

'More and more costs as prices decline. It is getting harder and harder to make a profit Jason, especially with the heavy rainfalls and regular flash flooding.'

There was no formal check-in at The Oaks North Ryde Suites,

a three-star hotel owned by another of Ravi's uncles. Jason accepted the key to a spartan single bedroom. In the restaurant tandoori, curry and pappadam aromas permeated the atmosphere. The two young men chatted while sharing plates of delicious food.

The next day, Jason ferried his young businessman to various meetings across the city, the last being at Parliament House. Ravi sighed as he alighted and reached into the back seat and extracted a cold Coke Zero from the car fridge. Jason squeezed the Benz into the heavy Friday afternoon traffic on Macquarie Street. As they cleared the city and settled onto the M1 Jason was eager to know more and to offer help if he could.

'Ravi, have you ever thought about growing other crops? Diversifying can help with your environmental problems and give you another income stream. You have all the infrastructure for cucumbers, passionfruit and herbs. And what about flowers. There's a lot of money for fresh flowers in Sydney. You're already growing marigolds. Why not scale it up?'

'We have so many problems to fix Jason and after today we have to fund a research project to measure nutrient levels in the two creeks for the next year.'

'Listen, my dad can help you with that Ravi? My father – Malcolm Withers. He'd love to use his knowledge and experience doing something useful instead of sitting at home in front of a computer complaining about the Liberal-National Party.'

They pulled into the Sidhu mansion well after midnight.

'You can sleep here tonight Jason. My sister has left clean pyjamas and underwear for you. You need a long sleep after all that driving. And why don't you bring your dad out on Sunday for lunch. We'd all like to meet him.'

◈

Malcolm was appalled when he witnessed the scale of destruction of his beloved forest and the extent of blueberry bushes. He couldn't believe the blankets of hideous plastic netting that covered the hills of previous pristine rainforest. Where were the stands of tall hardwood? Babbling creeks had been reduced to drains. Understory plants were completely absent, replaced by mown grass between the rows. It was an industrial wasteland on a scale unimaginable a decade ago.

Jason heard his dad's deep, soft voice above the noise of the motor.

The cold spring falls from the stone.
I paused and heard
the mountain, palm and fern
spoken in one strange word.
I peeled its splitting bark
and found the written track
of a life I could not read.

'Do you remember Judith Wright's poem *Scribbly Gum* Jason? There's no way I could have imagined it was this bad. How could they let this happen, all for some miserable blueberries. Don't people ever think about the cost?'

Jason knew that his father was referring to the value of the lost bush, not so much in dollar terms, but in biodiversity. Malcolm wrote endless letters to editors, councillors and parliamentarians about the wanton destruction of the North Coast forests. He received some replies but none placated his anger.

As the Camry came to a halt in front of the house, Jason scanned for wheelchair access. There was none, yet there were six steps to climb onto the spacious patio. Ravi came to meet them, his three sisters remaining on the patio.

The two young men carried Malcolm up the steps before Sirika insisted she push the wheelchair into the house, down the long, wide hallway and out into a majestic courtyard, the centre of which was a fountain. A table, set for lunch tucked away under shady Kentia Palms. Ravi's father, Ahmed, appeared and bowed to greet Malcolm. He was a tall, square-shouldered man who shook hands warmly with the two guests. The hip-length tailored Nehru jacket with high collar and yellow turban off-set his thick grey hair. His broad smile and welcoming words helped Malcolm and Jason relax in the formal setting.

The lunch was a banquet with bowl after bowl of scrumptious Indian food brought to the table by Aayra and the girls – so different from Malcolm and Jason's usual Sunday lunch of baked beans on toast. Ahmed sat next to Malcolm and the two men quickly became engaged in earnest conversation about the property, its history, the rainforest and the challenges of blueberry farming. Jason kept on eye on the older men, worried that his father might become angry with Ahmed.

But there was no need for him to worry. On the return journey Malcolm was upbeat about the prospect of Ahmed and his family changing their practices, considering regenerative farming and returning some of the land to its natural state.

'Ahmed is very keen to have koalas return to the property. He remembers them when he arrived here and they were considered pests. He seems to be seeking redemption for the environmental damage he's caused. Now that he has some wealth, he's in a position to try and turn things around. It's ironical that it takes all this time and destruction for a man to see the error of his ways. It may be too late, who knows.'

Under Malcolm's tutelage, Jason and the three girls planted herbs on the sunny side of the packing shed where seeds of basil, thyme, parsley and coriander had sprouted and were growing strongly. Jason and Sirika visited Coffs Harbour and Sawtell restaurants and touted the organically grown herbs. Fresh herbs delivered by a local, vibrant, young Indian woman was appealing to the chefs. It was the beginning of a lucrative trade and the herb garden expanded rapidly and profitably.

Jason spent more and more time with Sirika, not just working on the farm. Weekend drives took them to Bellingen for 'hippie' food as Jason referred to the vegetarian dishes of lentils, chickpeas and okra. Sirika loved exploring the village's boutique shops and often came away with clothes for herself and her sisters. She loved the Sunday markets and wondered why her family were not selling blueberries in their own stall. Everything that was harvested from their farm was packed away in boxes and sent to Sydney on a truck. They were not part of this vibrant community.

The ascent of the escarpment to Dorrigo always entranced Sirika, who marvelled at the dense rainforest with its massive eucalypts and the impressive tree ferns with gigantic green fronds. On the boardwalks she danced in delight above the olive-green canopy. Jason was hypnotised as Sirika spun dervish-like with her bright skirt splaying in afternoon sun and her long black hair trailing, so lithe, happy and unselfconscious. He had never met anyone like her. In her company, he felt free, bouyant and complete.

On a warm Sunday afternoon Jason drove deep into the National park and took Sirika to a secluded swimming hole. They frolicked, splashed and ducked each other in the cool water, Jason in his Billabong board shorts, Sirika in a yellow bikini that was stunning against her coffee-coloured skin. When she wrapped her long arms around his shoulders and her legs around his torso asking for a piggy back to the other side, Jason felt her skin press tightly to his back. He squeezed her thighs more closely to secure her and set off across the chest-deep water, aroused and pleased by her playful touching.

Afterwards, they dried each other with towels before dressing and setting off for home, arriving well after dusk. Sirika lent across to Jason and kissed him. Her lips lingered long enough to send a message to Jason that she was fond of him, not just as a friend, but maybe as a lover. The spare room was always available to him and when he did not need to attend to his father, he spent the night in the family home. Sirika began to make late evening visits and quietly slipped out of his bed before dawn.

Ahmed noticed the growing relationship between his daughter and Jason, a little worried by what other families would say about a non-Sikh dating their daughter. It was unusual for a Sikh girl to be so friendly with an Australian man. He spoke with his wife about the courtship.

'The Sunday drives should cease, Aarya, and Jason must not be allowed to sleep the night here. It was time Sirika embraced her Sikh community, especially the young men.'

Aayra retorted.

'It's too late for that Ahmed. Those two are becoming inseparable. Can't you see that? Sirika is very happy and it's time our eldest daughter thought about settling down and starting a family. They are a nice couple, well suited and Jason is very attentive towards Sirika. He is also a very good employee. Don't forget that Ahmed. He is an asset to our family.'

Ahmed was aghast. It was unthinkable that his daughter would marry a non-Sikh. He knew that such a marriage was acceptable if Jason adopted Sikh beliefs and practices, but he'd never considered it for any of his daughters. It worried him that many customs had already been eroded in this new country. The local Indian children were attending public schools, spending more and more time skate-boarding and less time at the temple and the religious events offered. Was it realistic, he wondered, to expect traditional ways to endure in a foreign land that had been so good for him and his family?

His own relationship with Malcolm was strong, but completely business like. The ex-forester was now providing advice and oversight of reclamation works. Ahmed was satisfied that a start had been made on planting riparian vegetation along the creeks and a system of mulching was now in place. His major objective of attracting koalas back to his property was taking longer. He expressed frustration to his advisor. Malcom was patient with his new boss but surprised by Ahmed's ignorance of habitat, ecology and koalas.

'Koalas will only eat the leaves of certain eucalyptus trees Ahmed. Because the original forest was clear-felled, it will take a few years to establish a colony again, but we've already planted 250 tallowwood, swamp mahogany and stringy bark, much like the original bush. Hopefully that will attract some koalas from the National Park to come and get a feed on the new leaves.'

Indigenous native trees, shrubs and ground covers were planted along the creek banks and began to attract honeyeaters, wattle birds and lorikeets. Composting began by mulching the pruned bushes and then spread to return nutrients to the soil. Over time fertiliser use declined, erosion was halted and run-off was reduced. The quality of the creek waters improved according to the university researchers. Progress had been made.

◆

Ravi began his studies at Bond University on the Gold Coast and leased a level 10 unit at Broadbeach with a view of the coast from Coolangatta to Stradbroke Island. In his Business Ethics

101 course he met many interesting students from around Australia, Asia and the Pacific. The topics covered intrigued him, and he listened with great interest to debates about sustainability, social licence and community engagement in business. He weighed these ideas with his father's blueberry business. Was the family meeting environmental regulation? What were the community's expectations? Was the family living up to ethical expectations of the twenty first century?

He did not contribute verbally to tutorial discussions, but listened intently and became impressed by another student who seemed to have plenty to say about businesses giving back to the community in which they operated. Michael Chan was from Malaysia and came to Bond on a scholarship. He was tall with thick black-rimmed glasses, possessed a confident demeanour and wore the same tight black jeans, scuffed sneakers and protest tee shirts every week. Ravi assumed that he was poor, despite his intelligence.

During the first term the pair became friendly and Ravi offered Michael free board at Broadbeach in exchange for company. Michael bought with him left-wing opinions, charm and hash plants. He also introduced Ravi to homosexuality. Ravi was still a virgin but he found Michael's sexual power and persuasion to be irresistible, especially after smoking a joint or two. By the end of term two the pair were an unmissable gay couple with twelve pots of cannabis sativa growing behind the sunny windows of their expensive apartment. Parties were being planned with Michael's gay friends. Subsequently, Ravi's academic performance plummeted. He'd failed Accountancy 101 and he'd dropped out of an elective, Australian History. Surprisingly he had not recorded a distinction or credit in the other subjects.

How could he possibly go home and face his father? It would be a walk of shame! Michael came to the rescue or so Ravi thought.

'No worries Ravi. Let's fly to my home in Kuala Lumpur and you can meet my parents.'

Ravi booked the business class tickets that night, paid for on his Amex Gold. He sent an email to his mother.

I've been invited by my friend to travel to Malaysia to meet his family this coming holiday. Michael's father is an executive with HSBC and I think it's a good opportunity to meet him. I've learnt at Uni that networking is very important in business. Who knows where it will lead?

Love you Mum, Ravi. xxoo

Ps hope everyone is going well down there. Say hello to Dad and the sisters.

Ravi and Michael were arrested at KL International Airport and each detained for importing 500 grams of hashish.

❖

Over time the Sidhu Blueberry Farm diversified and began to prosper. Sirika and her sisters, with Jason's advice and support, were empowered to develop other crops. A long greenhouse was established for growing flowers which were sent to the Sydney Flower Markets. The orchids, especially ones that were native to the North Coast became a premium product and provided a constant source of income. Below the dam another two greenhouses were constructed displacing blueberry bushes. Lebanese cucumbers thrived in the warm moist atmosphere and within months the family began to sell multiple pallet loads.

At Sirika's insistence the community was invited to come and 'Pick Your Own Blueberries' at the end of the season. With advice and support from a neighbouring organic dairy farm she began to make blueberry yogurt and ice-cream. Blueberry juice was produced. Aayra cooked the best blueberry muffins on the North Coast. The sisters booked a site at Bellingen markets and sold their products, meeting and mingling with interesting, friendly, helpful people.

Ahmed became deeply distressed at news that his son had received a sentence of five years confinement. Despite diplomatic efforts to have him returned to Australia, he remains incarcerated in a Kuala Lumper gaol. To help with Ahmed's depression Malcolm drove him to the Port Macquarie Koala Hospital. After making a sizeable donation, Ahmed was ushered into the enclosures and nursed an abandoned baby koala. The little one snuggled into his armpit while Ahmed stoked her soft fur. Tears rolled down his brown cheeks and he turned away from Malcolm and the staff, embarrassed at his unintended flow of tears.

Consequently there is now an adjunct Koala Rescue Hospital at the back of the Ahmed property to care for sick and injured koalas. Ahmed is funding the project and Aarya is the head of nursing. Community volunteers assist every day as the need grows. The furry, soft but wild koalas are released onto Sidhu land abutting the National Park.

◈

Jason and Sirika became engaged with the blessing of Aarya, Ahmed and Malcolm. A wedding is to be held at the family home after Jason accepted an invitation to become part of the Sikh faith. Aarya and her daughters are planning to cater for a feast with the assistance of other families. Two hundred and fifty people are expected to attend.